LOVE
Beyond
TIME

LOVE Beyond TIME

A Novel

NANCY CAMPBELL ALLEN

Covenant Communications, Inc.

Cover photo © *Lost Images,* Al Thelin

Published by Covenant Communications, Inc.
American Fork, Utah

Printed in the United States of America
First Printing: September 1999

06 05 04 03 02 01 00 99   10 9 8 7 6 5 4 3 2

ISBN 1-57734-540-1

To my parents, who always told me
I could achieve anything I wanted to

and

To my husband, who told me
to go ahead and do it.

"The laws of physics as we know them now don't disallow time travel . . . Anything that physics doesn't forbid must be considered."

—Dr. Paul Nahin, Professor, Electrical Engineering, University of New Hampshire. *Newsweek,* March 16, 1998.

Author's Note

This novel is a work of fiction. Dorothea Dix, Elizabeth Blackwell, Clara Barton, S. Weir Mitchell, and General Ulysses S. Grant are the only historical figures in this work. All other characters and their names are fictional and in no way reflect people, living or dead, who may bear the same or similar names.

General Stuart Tyler Montgomery is also a fictional character. He and his actions are unique to this book and are not intended to be a reflection, real or implied, of any historical figures influential during the American Civil War.

The battle in Chapter Nineteen is also fictional. In reality, Union troops were attacked by Confederates at Grand Junction, Tennessee, on December 20, 1862, but the Federals tallied only fifty casualties. The battle scene in this book was implied as a larger-scale conflict for purposes of the story line.

Chapter 1

The tension was thick in the small office. Tyler Montgomery's face was a barely controlled mask of fury. "I told you never to set foot in this office again. Either of you," he said through clenched teeth.

The two men each took a cautious step backward. "We, uh, we just came by to bring Derek his mail," one ventured hesitantly.

"Yeah, we were just leaving," mumbled the other. They scurried past him and were out of the room as quickly as they could manage.

Tyler looked at his friend with obvious concern. "Did they do anything to you?"

Derek sank wearily into a chair. "No. You know how they are, just a lot of hot air." He laughed. "Thanks. Again."

"Don't mention it." Tyler reached into his pocket and swore under his breath. "I must have left my wallet in the car." He left Derek's office and paused in the hall. "Lock your door if you have to." He turned and was gone.

Moments later, Kristina Montgomery appeared in Derek's doorway. "Where's Tyler?" she asked Derek breathlessly. "The secretary in the main office said he looked ready to kill someone."

Derek stood and motioned for her to come in. "He's fine," he said. "It's nice to see you again. He should be back in a minute. Do you want to wait for him in here?"

"Sure, that would be nice." She sat on a plush chair and looked carefully at Derek. "Are you okay? What happened up here?"

Derek sighed. "Those two little bigots from the mailroom showed up again. They were threatening me when Tyler walked in and . . . asked them to leave." He smiled. "They didn't need to be told twice."

"It seems like something along those lines was happening last time I was here," Kristina said. "Are you going to file a complaint?"

"Yes, for sure this time," Derek replied. Lost in his own thoughts, he shook his head.

Kristina sat in silence, contemplating the man before her. The reasons for her brother's actions were not a mystery to her. A legacy from his childhood, his utter disgust for bigotry ran bone-deep. She knew he had defended his co-worker not only because Derek was a good man, but because he was also an African-American. She knew that it was probably their father's face Tyler saw when he confronted people who were hopelessly ignorant and intolerant.

Kristina and Derek both turned at the knock on the office door. Derek opened it to let Tyler enter.

"The secretary said you were here," Tyler said, bending to give his sister a kiss on her cheek. "Do you need something, or just here to visit?"

"Here to visit," she replied, and rose to accompany him. She smiled at Derek and offered her hand. "It was good to see you, Derek. Take care."

"I will. You too," he replied.

Tyler was preoccupied as he and Kristina walked to his office. He closed the door firmly behind them and dropped into his chair, releasing a sigh.

Kristina sank down onto the sofa beneath a spacious window and looked closely at her brother. "It never ends, does it?" she asked.

He didn't have to ask what she meant. "No, it doesn't. Just when I think I have a life, something or someone reminds me of him."

Kristina shuddered at the unbidden image of her father that swam before her eyes. She swallowed the lump in her throat that occasionally formed when she considered her past, and Tyler's as well. She gave him a sad smile and thought of him as a child and adolescent—always trying to do exactly opposite of their father's wishes.

The old man had wanted Tyler to be an attorney, and never let him forget it, so Tyler had pursued every avenue possible to avoid that particular career. He participated in every sport and extracurricular activity he could find so that he wouldn't have time for whatever their father had planned for him.

Kristina shook off her musings and cleared her throat. "Do you want to go to dinner tonight? I think we both could use some company."

A look of regret crossed Tyler's features. "I can't, Kris. I have so much to do here. I probably won't be done before midnight. How about tomorrow?"

Kristina smiled at her handsome brother. His hair was dark brown, almost black, and his eyes were a beautiful hazel that twinkled on rare occasions when he allowed himself to be happy. He stayed physically active with running, swimming, and weight-lifting, more as mental therapy than conceit.

He'd made it to the ripe old age of thirty, and the fact that he was still single amazed her. She'd have thought some ambitious woman would have snatched him up before now. But then, he was too clever to allow himself to be snatched, she reminded herself. She wanted him to be happy, and doubted he would ever allow himself to become genuinely close to any woman. He didn't trust himself.

"Tomorrow will be fine," she said. "Call me, okay?"

"Okay." Tyler stood and allowed her to rumple his hair as she left. He sat back down at his desk and put his head in his hands. His head was pounding. It would be a long afternoon.

The hours melted rapidly together as Tyler sifted through stacks of papers and tapped patiently away on his computer keyboard, wondering a million times over why he'd stayed behind at work instead of enjoying a nice meal with his sister. He was nowhere near finished with the tasks before him; the company his firm was attempting to service was mired in an audit that would take nothing short of a miracle to emerge from unscathed.

Tyler rubbed his burning eyes and sighed. Had he been a bit more alert, he'd have reacted more quickly when his door suddenly flew open, and he was propelled violently from his chair and into the opposite wall by a vicious kick.

He barely registered the faces of the two men he'd ejected from Derek's office hours before. They apparently hadn't had the courage to face him earlier in the day when the office was teeming with people; it seemed they were more comfortable picking their battles under the cover of night and with weapons.

He blearily moved his arm in a feeble attempt to ward off the attack, but to no avail. The blow from the butt of the sawed-off shotgun to the side of his head was swift and sure. His last coherent thought was that he should have taken his sister up on her offer.

Chapter 2

Amber Saxton ran into her apartment, nearly colliding with her roomate. "Camille!" she laughed. "Sorry. I'm running late." She clutched a half-eaten bagel in one hand and struggled with an armload of books.

"Where are you going?" The bewilderment on Amber's roommate's face was apparent.

"I forgot I told Michelle I'd take her shift today, and I'm due in ER in about fifteen minutes," Amber quickly explained.

"Do you need a ride?" asked Camille.

"Could you? My car's still in the shop."

Life had been simpler when Amber and Camille had lived on campus. Success after graduation had moved them out of the city and into a more sedate area on the outskirts, but unreliable transportation was quickly becoming the bane of Amber's existence.

Amber grabbed her work clothes and on impulse snatched a book that was sitting forgotten on the couch as she made her way to the door. Camille smiled at the Primary 3 manual that was now crushed in Amber's arms.

"I guess you don't need me to sub for you this Sunday," Camille remarked with a smile.

"No, I should be okay this week. I'm not scheduled and I'm not on call, but you never can tell," Amber said. "Will you be around, just in case?"

"As always," Camille replied.

They reached the hospital, and Amber changed into her green scrub suit with minutes to spare. The flow was steady and Amber was on her feet, working amidst chaos for several hours into the night before she could take a small break. She relaxed in the doctors' lounge and sighed with contentment. At age twenty-five, she was already working hard at something she loved, and achieving goals she'd set for herself while still in her youth. She pulled a pen and some paper out of her cluttered, oversized purse and began a letter to her sister.

> *Dear Liz,*
>
> *I'm at work again, and I'm getting tired. It's so tempting to catch a few moments of sleep instead of faithfully telling you my innermost thoughts (ha ha), but I'm actually too keyed up to sleep now anyway. It's been a busy night. I find this stuff so fascinating. I love my residency and I know that I'm in the right field. There's rarely a dull moment in this place. I enjoy the variety in the emergency room and I've definitely chosen the profession for me. You know how bored I get with routine, so it's good for me to be somewhere that constantly moves and changes. Let me know when you get your computer up and running again. This snail-mail stuff has gotta go!*

Amber put her pen down and rubbed her eyes. Maybe she was tired enough to sleep for a little while. She rested her head on her arms and out of the corner of her eye, saw someone enter the room.

"Here, Amber, I brought you some food. You don't take care of yourself, so I came back to make you eat." Camille presented a packaged salad from the cafeteria, along with the ever-present plastic utensils and salad dressing pouch.

Amber smiled. "What would I do without you, Camille? You've been my guardian angel since kindergarten."

Camille grinned. "Aren't I great?"

"Wow! You even picked my favorite kind. Chef salad, turkey, no ham, lo-cal Italian dressing. Thanks. This is just what I needed," Amber said, stuffing a forkful of salad into her mouth. She washed the whole mess down with a long swig from the drink Camille had set in front of her. "Ahhh. You know me too well."

Camille grinned again and sank into a chair across from Amber. Tossing her long, black braids off her shoulder, she nodded her agreement. "I do indeed. One of these days I will break you of that nasty habit, but for now I'll let you indulge a bit."

"Well thank you, your royal-ness." The corner of Amber's mouth lifted in a self-deprecating smile. Camille was the healthiest person she knew, and Amber's caffeine addiction had been the topic of many a heated debate. She winked at her friend, noting for the millionth time, it seemed, the beautiful dark brown skin, the large chocolate brown eyes and engaging smile. "I have time to kick the habit, you know."

Camille snorted. "That's a lame excuse." She grinned. "Looks like I need to clean your purse out for you again, too. I had no idea a doctor could be such a slob."

Amber wrinkled her nose. "You organized people are so boring."

Camille laughed and turned her attention to the Primary manual Amber had deposited on the table. "Have you had a chance to look over your lesson yet?"

Amber shook her head, her mouth full. "I'll do it when I finish my letter to Liz," she finally said when she swallowed. "Didn't you do the lesson on 'Kindness to Animals' last week?"

Camille nodded and opened her mouth to reply when they were interrupted by a hospital aide who burst into the room. "Dr. Saxton, they need you right away. Gunshot wound. Room One."

Amber stood and wiped her mouth. "Come along for the ride?" she asked Camille on her way out the door. The dubious expression on Camille's face contradicted her actions as she followed her friend down the hall and into the emergency section. The area was flooded with people who were moving quickly and giving orders as the stretcher was wheeled into place.

"What happened?" Amber asked the paramedic who ran alongside the victim.

"Gunshot wound to the abdomen. Blood pressure is ninety over fifty and falling," he answered.

Camille stood on the fringes of the activity, fascinated but concerned about her presence being intrusive. She was standing by the room's swinging doors to keep a safe distance when she noticed a man standing uncomfortably close to the stretcher.

"You need to get out of the way, sir," one of the doctors in the room told him brusquely.

The man looked sick. "I just want to make sure he's okay," he mumbled. "I went back to work to get some things and I found him in his office, passed out on the floor. His name is Tyler Montgomery." He swallowed. "I can't figure it out. Someone shot him in the stomach. And he's dressed weird . . ."

"What's your name?" Amber asked the man as he was shoved farther away from the stretcher.

"Derek Bradford. I . . . I work with him," was his reply.

"Why don't you take him somewhere, Camille," Amber suggested. "Get some fresh air."

"The police officer said she wanted to talk to me." Derek looked hesitant and made no move to leave.

"Tell her we're in the cafeteria," Camille said to Amber as she grabbed Derek's hand and pulled him from the room. "Come on, I'll buy you something to drink."

Amber glanced at the patient on the stretcher and raised her eyebrows as she held her hands up in front of her face so the attending nurse could slip the snug medical gloves onto them. The gunshot victim was, without a doubt, the best-looking man she'd ever seen. "What business does such a clean-cut guy have getting himself shot?" she said aloud.

The chief resident shrugged as he quickly attended to the patient. "I'm wondering what he's wearing. Looks like he's been to a costume party or something."

Amber looked again and noticed what seemed to be a genuine reproduction of a Civil War Confederate Army uniform. Her brows drew together in a frown as she worked alongside the other physician. "His friend said he was in an office," she said, puzzled. She turned her attention to other matters with a wry expression. "Why are we so understaffed all of a sudden?"

"Our two delinquent interns disappeared," he answered her, clearly frustrated. "I wouldn't be using them at all except that Jones, Felsted, and Collins all called in sick." As though on cue, two young men rushed into the room.

"Sorry," one offered. "Where do you want us?"

"In law school," muttered the chief resident. Amber snorted.

"Huh?"

"Nothing. Come here and take Amber's place," said the chief resident. "Her break was cut short and she's been on this shift longer than you two combined. We've got to get this guy stabilized and then prep him for surgery."

"I'm okay, really," Amber said. For some reason she couldn't fathom, she hated to leave the still form whose wound was bleeding profusely. His vital signs were dangerously low. She shook her head at the ironies of life. Here was a healthy-looking guy, one who reminded her of a dark-haired Greek god, and he was barely alive.

The chief resident's voice broke her train of thought. "Amber, you still have a few hours left and it's late. Go rest for a minute. I'll holler if I need you."

Amber walked slowly toward the lounge, then stopped to gaze in the direction of the emergency room she had just left. Her brows were drawn in a bemused frown, and she had to force herself to continue her journey back to her half-eaten salad and Primary manual. As she turned toward the lounge again, gnawing her lower lip in confusion, she walked directly into a door being shoved open in haste.

As she slowly crumpled to the floor, she saw enough stars to rival any childhood cartoon and heard a horrified gasp that sounded far away.

"I hit Dr. Saxton in the head with the door! Someone help me . . ." The voice droned on incoherently as Amber's vision faded entirely to blackness.

Chapter 3

Tyler awoke feeling groggy. He must have fallen asleep at the desk in his office. He shook his head. That was odd. He never slept at work. As he stretched, he smelled the pungent aroma of a kerosene lamp. The light coming from outside appeared to be fading, and the lamp offered little help.

Something was very wrong. He was on the floor. With a sudden swiftness, he remembered being attacked by the two men from the mailroom. He raised a shaky hand to his head and felt the unmistakable lump from the shotgun butt. His eyes slowly surveyed the room. Instead of his desk, computer, and small couch, he saw two beds and two desks. He looked at the floor, which should have been adorned by plush, cream-colored carpet; instead he found hardwood planks.

He slowly stood and walked over to one of the beds in confusion, examining the faded patchwork quilt that lay neatly folded upon it. Apparently, the two idiots hadn't been content with assault and battery. They'd abducted him, as well.

Trying to make sense of his surroundings, Tyler looked up at the dim light entering the room from the small window. There was a knock at the door. "Come in!" he barked, wincing at the noise he'd generated. The door slowly opened, and a young boy of fifteen or so ventured uncertainly inside.

"Hello, sir," he stammered. "I wasn't sure if you were here. No one saw you arrive." The boy looked Tyler up and down, taking in the white shirt, tie, dress slacks, and immaculate shoes. "Do you not have a uniform?" he asked. "If you'd like, I can go now and get whatever you need from supplies."

Tyler was on the boy in a flash. He grabbed him by the neck and slammed him into the wall. "I don't find any of this funny in the least," he said, his voice dangerously low. "Why don't you just relay this message for me. You tell those two racist bigots that not only will they face jail time for this, I'll personally see to it that they suffer. Now, you go tell them that I am not amused."

The boy was clearly frightened. "I . . . I . . . don't know what you mean, sir. I was told that the old accountant finally died of typhoid and that a new one was coming to take his place. Your regiment will be in the area soon, and you'll meet up with them when they get here."

Tyler released the boy and stared at him. "What are you talking about?"

The boy squirmed uncomfortably. "Perhaps you'd rather speak to the colonel." He turned and ran from the room. Tyler slowly followed him out the door and turned to his left. He stared in disbelief at the sight before him.

I've died and I'm not in heaven, he thought as he looked at a long, narrow room with beds down either side and an old-fashioned wood-burning stove in the middle. The floor was wooden, as was the ceiling, which came to a peak at the top. There were large kerosene lamps approximately twelve feet above the floor, suspended from studs that crossed from one wall to the opposite side.

Tyler turned around and looked to his right, only to see the scene repeated before him. When the stench of the place fully assailed his nostrils, he recognized the odor as a mixture of alcohol and bodily filth. He heard soft moaning coming from the beds. His eyes widened a bit as he stepped closer and saw rows and rows of what appeared to be wounded people. Some had bandages around their heads and faces, others were missing an arm or leg. Some slept, while others who were conscious looked miserable.

"Young man?" Tyler jumped at the voice. He turned around to see a man dressed in a full Civil War Union Army uniform.

"I'm Colonel Duncan. I'm the commanding officer here," the man stated, his gaze slowly traveling the length of Tyler's body as though viewing an oddity. "How long have you been in the Army, son?"

Tyler's head was pounding. Surely this was a prank. The two mail-room idiots had somehow managed to ship him to some sort of play-acting camp. He'd heard of Revolutionary War reenactment scenarios; apparently a Civil War arena had been created as well.

"I said, how long have you been in the Army?" the man before Tyler repeated his question.

"Actually, I was in the Navy, sir," Tyler replied truthfully. "I served overseas, mostly, off the coast of Japan." *Two can play at this,* he mused to himself with a measure of spite. When he caught up with those responsible for his abduction, they'd never know what hit them.

Tyler shifted under the "colonel's" skeptical gaze and avoided the man's eyes; something he normally never did. He couldn't place a finger on the source of his discomfort.

"I understand you met Boyd, and I'd thank you to treat him kindly in the future. That boy just lost his father and two brothers to this wretched war. He'll be back shortly with a uniform for you." The colonel turned to leave and suddenly turned back.

"Oh," he said. "I don't believe I know your name, son."

"Stuart Tyler Montgomery VI, U.S. Navy, sir," Tyler replied dutifully.

The colonel came to stand mere inches away from Tyler's face, and he sensed the urgency and seriousness in the older man's voice.

"I don't know exactly what it is you're up to, Montgomery, but let me tell you something," said the colonel. "This country is tearing itself apart. There are sixteen Union Army hospitals here in the Washington D.C. area alone, and every single one is full to capacity. Why, we even have wounded being cared for in the House and Senate chambers, the Georgetown Jail, and the Patent Office.

"I have seen more boys die in here than I can count, and I don't have time to play games with you. I was given to understand we'd have an Army man here to serve as a new accountant. If you're not certain which branch of the military you've been serving in, then perhaps we should have you committed to an institution for the mentally insane. Now then, Mr. Montgomery, what is your *Army* rank, or do you even have one?"

The first stirrings of desperate unease began to manifest themselves as Tyler stared in response to the man's outburst. Something was horribly, frighteningly wrong. He found himself beseeching a God he didn't believe in to make the whole odd situation disappear.

"I'm sorry, sir. I'm a captain," he lied, stammering. What was going on? He gazed, transfixed at the man standing opposite him and regarded the kind yet tired face, the graying hair, and the short stature. The man was an effective actor. Tyler sensed his exhaustion as though it were a tangible thing.

He spied a door that he hoped would lead to the world outside. If he could just make it to the door, he'd see and hear the hustle and chaos of the city. Keeping the colonel in his sight, he made his way to the door, and upon reaching it, flung it open with a vengeance. The sight before him wrung a groan of frustration from his lips.

Venturing outside, Tyler realized that he was either on a set of a Washington D.C. Civil War reenactment camp, or that the impossible had occurred. The second possibility didn't warrant contemplation from a man who'd lived his entire life grounded in harsh reality. Perhaps, if he just played along, he'd be allowed to return home.

He turned at the sound of approaching footsteps.

"Are you ill, Captain?" asked the colonel.

Tyler sucked in several gulps of fresh air and willed himself to remain standing. "I think I'll go back in the bedroom and wait for Boyd," Tyler murmured, his apprehension mounting with each passing moment.

The colonel saluted. "Very well. I'll expect to see you at 1800 hours for dinner. It's just in the next building over," he said, pointing. He paused for a moment in reflection. "Did you say your name was Stuart Tyler Montgomery?"

"Yeah," Tyler muttered. "The sixth."

"Are you familiar with Stuart Tyler Montgomery, the Army general?" asked the colonel. "In fact, I'm sure you must be aware that it's his regiment you'll be joining up with in about a week."

Tyler stared for a long moment before answering, his anger mounting. "No, *sir*. I wasn't aware of that."

"Well, Captain, do you at least have your transfer orders with you? Any proof of identification at all?"

Tyler was furious. "Well, you know," he spat with sarcastic energy born of fatigue and rage, "I was in an accident not too long ago, one involving a fall from my horse. I was out surveying the area, searching for old Johnny Reb, and the next thing I knew I was on the ground and my horse had taken off! Must have hit my head pretty hard, because I haven't remembered much since then!"

The colonel gave Tyler a long, hard look and said, "I'll see what I can do for you, Captain." He gave one more backward glance at Tyler's clothes and was gone.

Chapter 4

Amber heard the buzzing voices before she opened her eyes. Her head was spinning and she wondered why she felt as though she'd been hit with a two-by-four. She sat up and looked at her watch. It had stopped. She rubbed her eyes and stretched, wondering why no one had come to get her. And why was she on the floor?

It wasn't until she thoroughly absorbed her surroundings that she realized something was wrong. She was in a small room containing two beds and a small table, lit by kerosene lamps. She was awfully tired. Maybe she'd moved to a different room and didn't remember. Except that this room was one she'd never seen.

The voices grew louder and the door suddenly opened. Two women wearing plain, ankle-length black dresses with unadorned white pinafores entered the room. They stopped abruptly when they spied Amber, clearly surprised by her presence.

"Another new nurse?" one asked. She turned to the other woman and said, "I thought you were our only new one this month."

Amber stood and rubbed a hand across her eyes. She didn't have time for nonsense. Who knew how long she'd slept? The chief resident was probably looking for her.

"Actually, maybe you can help me," she said wearily. "I'm a little confused. I must be in the wrong place." She stopped speaking as the women looked at her, open-mouthed. She looked down at her green scrub suit and white smock. "What?" she asked. "What's wrong?"

"I've never seen such ridiculous, outlandish clothing in all my life! Why, it's not even decent!" said one of the women.

Amber raised her eyebrows. "Would you mind telling me where I am so I can get back to work, please." It was more of a command than a request. Due to the demanding nature of her career and the fast pace she followed, she'd become accustomed to people following her orders. "I don't think I've ever been in this corner of the hospital."

The two women exchanged glances, and neither spoke for a moment. Finally, the one who seemed to be in charge stepped forward. "Are you a nurse?" she asked. "Did Miss Dix send you here?"

Amber sighed impatiently, smacking at her watch with her forefinger. The battery must have died. "I'm a doctor. A second-year resident."

The women stared at her as though she was crazy. "Are you an associate of Miss Blackwell?" asked the one who had taken charge of the conversation.

"Miss Blackwell? Elizabeth Blackwell?" Amber's eyebrows were raised high. "I can't call her that, exactly."

"Well, what would you call her?" The woman looked at her intently.

"I'd call her my hero, since I was about nine," Amber said impatiently. " Listen, I *really* don't have time for this . . ."

The second woman ventured a question. "Who is Elizabeth Blackwell?"

Amber looked at her. How could any woman entering the medical profession *not* know of Elizabeth Blackwell? "She was only the first woman to become a doctor in the United States," Amber stated, running a hand through her hair and rubbing her tired eyes. "She was admitted to college as a joke and graduated at the top of her class in 1849. No hospitals would hire her, so she started her own clinic in New York. Then in 1868, she opened a medical college for women, until women were finally allowed to attend medical school in . . . 1899."

As she ended her recitation of the pertinent facts on Elizabeth Blackwell, she noticed the shocked expressions on the women before her.

The first woman cleared her throat. "How, exactly, do you know she opened a college in 1868?"

Amber bristled at the woman's tone. "I had a class on the history of women in medicine. I read about it a long time ago."

"Today's date is October 16, 1862. Do you see the future, Miss . . . ," questioned the first woman.

Amber's eyes narrowed a fraction. "Saxton. *Doctor* Saxton." She looked closely at the first woman, then the second. "This is ridiculous."

She stormed past the women and out of the room, but stopped short outside the door and looked around, her eyes huge. She saw the rows and rows of wounded, heard the moaning, and smelled the stench of death and decay.

She bolted back into the room with the women and slammed the door. "What is this?" she asked, her fists clenched and her face flushed. "What is this?" she repeated, shrieking.

"Sit down, dear, just sit down and relax," said the woman who had questioned Amber as she took her arm and led her to one of the beds. "You must try to settle down. The patients need their rest. Now, we've all been under an enormous amount of stress, what with the war and all, and—"

"War? What war?" Amber felt sick to her stomach. She was so very tired. The long hospital hours hadn't affected her adversely before, but perhaps they were finally taking their toll.

The women retreated to the far corner of the room. "Perhaps she's one of those mad women, you know, deranged?" suggested the second. Their hushed voices broke through Amber's stupor.

"Yes. There are asylums, you know," agreed the first. "Perhaps we should notify someone of her presence here. With everything else going on, we certainly don't need someone like this to worry about."

Amber bolted from the room and rushed down the length of the outer area until she came upon the first visible door. Yanking it open with a force that nearly tore it from its hinges, she ran outside and didn't stop until she was near collapse.

Her breath came in sobbing gasps. Nothing was as it should have been. She recognized the lay of the land, but the city itself was all wrong. There were buildings that should have looked old, but were new. There were houses and structures that she'd never seen before. And the people. She recognized men wearing what must have been genuine reproductions of Civil War Union Army uniforms and women dressed in long, full, elaborate dresses that the country hadn't seen for well over a century.

Her first explanation was that she'd been dropped in the middle of an elaborate movie set. But the farther she ran, the more panicked she became as she realized that the set never ended. Her world was not beyond the borders of the old city. There were no borders.

Her pace eventually slowed, and she wandered aimlessly about what *should* have been Washington D.C. at the end of the twentieth century. Gnawing on her lower lip with enough intensity to draw blood, she elicited more than a few stares from passersby.

She couldn't formulate the words to a prayer. *Please help me, please help me* . . . was all she was able to think as one foot continued in front of the other. Finally, she found herself standing at her point of origin outside the odd infirmary.

Her heart in her throat, tears dangerously threatening, she made her way back inside. She walked to the room where she'd left the two startled women and entered mechanically. Amazingly enough, they were still there.

The women stared as Amber closed the door quietly and leaned against it. "Where am I?" she asked of them in a hoarse, angry whisper. The woman who had quizzed Amber prior to her hasty departure pulled a chair over to the bed and led her to it, sitting opposite her and regarding her carefully. "My name is Katherine Hill," she said. "I'm in charge of the nurses here at this hospital." Her voice was calm, the brown eyes kind. "Can you please tell me who you are?"

"I . . . I . . ." Amber closed her eyes and the tears spilled over. What to say? "My name is Amber Saxton," she managed on a wavering sob.

The woman took Amber's hand between her own and rubbed comfortingly. "How did you come to be here, Amber?" She eyed Amber's clothes again. "And where, exactly, are you from?"

The lie came easily, considering the frayed state of her nerves. "I am from a small island," she cleared her throat, "just off the coast of South America." She held her breath, hoping she wouldn't have to offer details about exact locations. The women were still eyeing her expectantly.

Amber wiped a tear and continued. "Where I come from, women can freely go to medical school if they want to, and . . ." she gulped, hoping she sounded convincing, "and dress this way. I suppose I came here to volunteer my services . . ." She trailed off and tried to smother the sob that erupted from her throat.

"Oh, you poor thing!" Katherine sighed. "Have you no desire to return home, Amber? This country is not very pleasant these days."

"Actually, I would love to return home, but I don't know when that will be possible. It seems to be very much out of my hands." Amber sniffed and accepted the handkerchief she was offered.

Katherine was sympathetic. "Yes, and I'm sure you don't want to get on another ship." She paused. "Did you travel by ship?"

"Yes?" *Ship. Would I have traveled by ship?* "Yes." The answer was more definitive.

"Well, assuming you're qualified, I'm sure we could use your services here. We need all the help we can get. I'll find a proper uniform for you, and, well, we'll have to pin up that hair of yours." Katherine took a closer look at Amber's thick, chestnut-colored hair that fell down past her shoulders in curled waves. She paused and leaned closer to Amber. "Well, if you're not an associate of Elizabeth Blackwell, you must be under the jurisdiction of Miss Dix. Dorothea Dix is the head of all the Union Army nurses. I'm afraid in your case, we're breaking some of her rather stringent rules."

Amber nodded through teary eyes. Ah yes. The rules. The class that had broadened her education of Elizabeth Blackwell had done the same regarding Dorothea Dix. She had forgotten the details.

"Miss Dix does not generally allow anyone under thirty years of age to serve as a Union Army nurse." Katherine paused. "How old are you, dear?"

"I'm twenty-five."

Katherine Hill pursed her lips. "She also prefers plain-looking women. Just, well, try not to smile too much or encourage any attention. I'll speak to Miss Dix about employing you when she returns to town."

Amber swallowed past the painful lump in her throat. "Ms. Hill, I shall do my very best to be unobtrusive." *Extremely unobtrusive,* she thought to herself and fought another wave of panic.

Katherine turned to leave, and as an afterthought, turned back and said, "Amber, you may not want to mention the fact that you're trained as a doctor. Some of the doctors here, well, they have a hard enough time working with the female nurses as it is. For your sake, I suggest you pose as a nurse."

For the first time in her life Amber realized she wasn't in a position to argue, so she merely nodded. Katherine turned to the other woman and said, "Well, Janet, it looks as though you already have a roommate." She turned to Amber and said, "Janet is new here also. She has been a nurse for many years, and you would do well to watch and behave as she does."

Katherine smiled at Amber. "I'm sure the nurses do things differently here than they do in your country. Well, I'll leave you now to get acquainted while I see what I can do about finding a proper uniform for you. I'm afraid that what you're wearing now will *never* do. Dinner will be in thirty minutes."

Chapter 5

Tyler was sitting on the bed with his head in his hands when Boyd knocked and entered, holding a bundle of neatly folded clothing. "Sir?" He approached hesitantly. "I have your uniform."

"Boyd, what year is it?" Tyler asked.

"Sir?"

"Tell me what year this is supposed to be, please," Tyler repeated.

"It's 1862, sir." Boyd hesitated. "Would you like to try your uniform on now?"

Tyler studied the boy for a moment. It wouldn't hurt to have an ally. "Yes, I suppose I should get into uniform. We don't want to be late for dinner now, do we?"

Tyler unconsciously clenched his jaw when Boyd left the room. He hated having to depend on anyone but himself.

They arrived at the mess hall precisely on time, and Tyler followed Boyd's movements, trying to be inconspicuous. He nodded to Colonel Duncan and sat down to a dinner of corn, biscuits, and beans.

He was trying to concentrate on the meal before him when a woman in the food line dropped her tray on the floor. He glanced up at the noise to see the woman staring straight at him. "I know you," she called out, her voice wavering as she left the food line. She was abruptly hauled back by two other women.

She pulled against their restraining hands and began a desperate attempt to free herself. "Let me go!" she shouted at the women. "I know him!"

Before Tyler could react, they pulled her from the building.

"Montgomery. His name is Montgomery . . ." Although the door had been hastily closed, her voice was discernible to Tyler inside.

"Who was that woman, Boyd?" Tyler asked, his eyebrows knitted in a frown as he rose.

"I don't know, sir. I've never seen her before," Boyd replied.

"Excuse me." Tyler left his tray sitting on the table. He walked quickly, increasing speed so that by the time he left the building he was running. Where had she gone? He rushed around the perimeter of the mess hall, the neighboring buildings and the surrounding area but could find no trace of the woman or her companions. With a stifled curse, he retraced his steps and began his search all over again.

****

"Amber, really! I thought we agreed you'd stay quiet and inconspicuous!" said a flustered Katherine, who had physically dragged Amber back to her room. "If you continue, someone will have you committed to an institution immediately! Now, I'm trying to help you here. You *cannot* harass the men!"

Amber was completely frustrated herself. She was certain she had just seen the man from the stretcher at the hospital.

"I know I've seen that man before, and I never forget a face," she said emphatically. *Especially one like that*, she thought to herself.

She shook her head and rubbed her temples, a small moan escaping her lips. She couldn't make sense of the fact that she'd apparently jumped approximately 137 years back in time. The long dress she wore was awkward, heavy, and felt completely foreign. Janet, her quiet new roommate, had arranged her hair in a bun common for the day, and it felt strange on her head.

Katherine smoothed Amber's pinafore and tucked a stray hair back into place. She shrugged. "I've never seen him before. He may be new, you know. We get people going in and out of here all the time." She patted Amber's shoulder. "There. Are you composed?"

Amber nodded.

"Good. Now then, let's go back and try to eat this time," she suggested. "You'll need all your strength, Amber. We may be busy tonight."

Amber swallowed the bland dinner and stole glances at the officers seated at the next table. The man she thought she knew was gone. *Pull yourself together, Amber,* she told herself repeatedly. *Finish your dinner and you can go looking for him*. Having promised Katherine she wouldn't make another scene, she tried to study the room as casually as possible. Tyler Montgomery. That was his name. She remembered his friend had brought him into the hospital and described the situation in which he'd found his colleague.

****

Tyler happened upon the woman by chance. She was in what he presumed was a supply building, receiving instruction from one of the women he'd seen her with earlier. Perhaps the screaming woman was all part of the elaborate play in which he'd become enmeshed; that would explain the reason she knew his name. He needed to talk to her . . . alone. Women were easy targets for him. He'd have the answer from her in no time.

The older nurse finally left the building, and Tyler slipped in unnoticed. He observed the woman, who remained oblivious to his presence. *Finally*, he thought to himself. He'd been searching for well over an hour. He cleared his throat, unsure of where to begin.

Amber whirled around at the unexpected sound and stared at Tyler. He watched the emotions flit across her face—recognition, confusion, and finally anxiety. She was as easily read as a book.

"You mentioned that you know me," he began, watching her carefully. What if she was in the same predicament he was? Maybe he was losing his mind.

He studied her intently. Her hair was parted in the middle and gathered in a bun at the back of her head, and she wore a plain black dress and white apron. The fringe of bangs on her forehead framed her nervous eyes, making them appear enormous in her face that was pale beneath her tan.

Fringe of bangs? In all the pictures he'd ever seen of the time period, he'd never noticed a haircut like that. A tan? He thought nineteenth-century women had supposedly fainted dead away at the thought of too much exposure to the sun. Whoever was responsible for casting the actors hadn't done his research.

He glanced at the hand fisted in the sheet she held. A class ring sparkled in the dim light. He smirked and approached her, lifting her hand and examining the date fashioned around the diamond. The whole thing was an elaborate charade. She'd forgotten to take off her class ring before stepping into her role as a Civil War nurse.

"High school or college?" he asked.

"College." Amber's breath came out on a ragged sigh. "I knew I'd seen you before." Her knees buckled and she sank to the floor. He followed her, grateful for the excuse to sit. The trauma of the whole situation had left him feeling weak.

"You're Tyler Montgomery," she finally said.

"Yes." He paused, taking a deep breath. "Now how is it that you know me, but I've never met you? Are you in league with the two bigots?"

Her brow wrinkled in confusion. "I'm a second-year resident at George Washington. A few hours ago, I think, I was at work in the ER, and you came in with a gunshot wound. You were wearing a Civil War uniform, a Confederate one, and a man you work with said he found you passed out in your office . . ." Her voice trailed off as he shook his head.

"That's never happened to me. I don't have any idea what any of this is all about, and I think you know that. What I *do* know is that I was attacked in my office by two men, and they apparently brought me here to this Civil War play-place. I have no idea why, but I'm done now, and I'd like to leave. I'm thinking you're the one to help me." His calm voice masked his agitation, his gaze was cool and unwavering.

She stared. "Are you insane?" she finally managed. "This isn't some 'play-place' and I have nothing to do with any of it! When I got here I took off running, and I'm telling you, it's for real. It goes on forever. I *know* Washington D.C. This is it; it's just not the right year. And I'll tell you what else is real," she said as he narrowed his eyes. "Those wounded men in the infirmary. Whatever else this place may be, that much is authentic."

He examined her face for any signs of insincerity or falsehood. Her eyes were red-rimmed; evidence of tears that he, himself, could end up shedding if what she was saying was true. Her eyes were a startling green. They stared back at him, huge and terrified. There was no doubt in his mind that she believed the things she was saying.

"I'll show you," she whispered. She stood and reached for a heavy cloak that she wrapped herself in before turning and extending her hand to him where he still sat on the floor.

He finally accepted it and stood, opening the door and allowing her to exit before him. He'd humor her. Maybe he'd see something she hadn't noticed. It was dark outside, certainly darker than he'd ever known the city to be, even in the middle of the night. The bright twentieth-century city lights were notably absent.

The doctor clung to Tyler's hand as she quickly led the way out of the area, glancing to the left and right to be sure they weren't being watched. They walked along in silence, the scenery speaking for itself. They traversed streets, peering in some buildings and entering others that were open, taking in every detail of the surroundings.

They had walked in the brisk fall air for a few miles before she said anything. "Well?" was all she asked.

"Well what? We could be out in the middle of the country some-where. I still say this is all some kind of movie set or something."

She stopped walking and looked at him. "Are you serious? We've been walking for miles! If this place is a set, it's enormous!"

"It could happen. I just saw a movie about a guy whose whole life was lived in a bubble, and he never even knew his world was a false one." Tyler began to feel the desperate panic of one grasping at straws.

"Oh!" Amber sat down where she stood and put her head in her hands. They had reached a quiet residential area and were thankfully able to converse unobserved.

Tyler squatted down next to her on the ground and touched her arm. "What's wrong with you?" he asked, almost warily. He knew nothing about the woman beside him, except that she claimed to be a physician, was out of her element, and appeared to collapse at the slightest provocation. He was taken aback when she raised her head, her eyes flashing and her expression fierce.

"You're living in an extremely happy place, mister, if you think for one minute this is something that's going to go away if we just walk far enough." Her words were clipped. "I have no idea what's happen-ing, but I do know that if we walk far enough in a southern direction, we'll probably stumble across a battle. If we head west, we'll eventual-ly come across a largely uninhabited frontier, until we hit a bunch of mining towns on the west coast!"

Her eyes were narrowed and she spoke with a fierceness that matched his own on a good day. Perhaps he'd misread her. She wasn't weak; she'd merely been dealing with facts that he hadn't wanted to face since waking up in the small bedroom at the hospital.

As his worst speculations were confirmed, Tyler moved from a crouched position facing the woman to sit beside her. He remained silent for a long moment before attempting to speak.

"You can't be sure," he whispered.

"Oh, but I am."

"How?"

"Can't you feel it? It's not the same. We're not home."

He knew it to be true. He put his head in his hands, much the same way she had when she initially sank to the ground. His breath came in short, painful gasps, and he felt overwhelmingly dizzy.

"Here," she said briskly, pulling at his leg. "Put your head between your knees."

He did as she ordered and managed to slow his erratic breathing while she patted his back as she would a small child, murmuring soothing words of calm and comfort. When he finally raised his head, he found her green eyes gazing at him, nearly glowing in the darkness.

"It'd be a lot easier to pretend it's just a joke, wouldn't it?" she said seriously.

"It is a joke," he answered harshly. "A sick one that I'm not getting."

She sighed, her hand still on his back. "I don't get it either. I've read everything Stephen Hawking has ever written—this just isn't supposed to happen."

"I happen to have seen a PBS special or two myself," he said, rubbing his eyes. "Apparently, Dr. Hawking has overlooked something."

"I suppose the question now is, what are we going to do?"

It was the first time in his life that he didn't have a ready answer to a dilemma. He shrugged.

"Well, I've been put to work as a nurse," Amber said. "What are you supposed to be doing here? Who have you talked to?"

Tyler sighed. "They think I'm an accountant here to replace one who just died, and I'm supposed to be joining up with a regiment whose general is, apparently, one of my ancestors." The irony wasn't lost on him. He'd finally escaped the clutches of his own father, only to be thrown further back into his family tree. He glanced at the woman seated beside him. "I don't even know your name."

"Amber Saxton." Her voice was soft. The brisk wind gently lifted some strands of hair that had come loose from the bun at the back of her head. Her eyes wore the exhaustion borne of despair and fatigue; he imagined they were a mirror of his own. "Promise me something," she whispered.

He nodded, anticipating her request. Had she not said it first, he knew he would have.

"Don't leave me."

The solitary pair sat in the darkness for several long moments before finally standing and making the long walk back to the Union Army Hospital.

Chapter 6

Tyler tossed and turned, exhausted but too agitated to sleep. His practical, logical, cynical mind simply could not accept what was happening. He stood and pressed his forehead against the window, enjoying the feel of the cool glass against his skin.

He took in the scene before him, looking out into the hospital area with its many small buildings. Most were dark, but some glowed with light from within. He realized sleep was going to remain elusive at best; and was most likely impossible if he gave the matter truthful consideration. He decided a walk in the brisk air might help clear his thoughts and considered asking his newfound doctor-friend to come along.

He opened her bedroom door a crack and viewed her form, huddled defensively on her bed. The even sounds of her breathing and rise and fall of her shoulder indicated to him that she'd been able to capture that which had remained tantalizingly out of his reach. Slumber, at his current station, was a commodity he'd have greedily purchased with his last dime.

He closed Amber's door with a soft sigh and exited the infirmary, heading out toward the other buildings that were lit. As he reached the first, the sounds coming from inside piqued his curiosity and bid him to enter, and the sight he encountered made him wish he hadn't.

He had apparently found some sort of operating or surgery room. He stood in the doorway, unable to tear his eyes away from the sight of a soldier in the process of having his leg removed. He was unaware of Colonel Duncan's approach and blinked when the older man stepped into his line of vision.

"I said, Captain, are you feeling well?" Colonel Duncan repeated himself.

"I . . ." Tyler cleared his throat. "I was just out for a walk. I didn't know what this was, really . . ." His voice trailed off.

Duncan eyed him speculatively. "I could use a strong hand or two. Do you think you have the stomach for it?"

"I'm not much of a surgeon, sir."

"I know," Duncan replied. "We have to do some amputating, and the patients sometimes get a little distraught. Most are braver than they should ever have to be, but some get frantic as they consume more alcohol. If you could just stay close by in case we need someone to help us hold them down, I would appreciate it. We're running short on medical staff."

Tyler took another good look at the room. There were puddles of blood on the floor and tables. His stomach turned at the smell. The men were moaning in pain, and many were drinking whiskey as quickly as they could in preparation for impending amputations.

Duncan noticed Tyler's obvious discomfort and took pity on him. "You'll get used to it, son." He shook his head. "Believe it or not, this actually becomes routine." He motioned with his head for Tyler to follow him to a table where a man was struggling incoherently with the two surgeons attending him. "Hold his shoulders," Duncan instructed Tyler, while he placed his hands around the soldier's ankles.

Tyler watched in fascinated horror as one of the doctors before him grabbed the man's head to hold it steady while the other forced the man's chin down and placed a white cloth over the patient's open mouth. He then began to drop a liquid onto the cloth and held the mouth open to insure the patient breathed in the fumes of the liquid.

"What is that stuff?" Tyler asked the colonel.

"Ether. It renders the patient unconscious so we can amputate," he answered.

The patient on the table eventually relaxed, and Tyler dropped his jaw as one of the surgeons produced a crude-looking saw. It took all of his strength to keep from running from the room. The sound, the smell, and the image of the soldier's face burned into his mind, forever seared into his memory, as if he had not already endured enough in his life. He looked at the suffering around him and, as he often had before, scoffed at the notion of a benevolent God.

"Why don't you go sit down for a while. I'll call you if I need you again." Colonel Duncan's voice broke through Tyler's thoughts.

Tyler turned and walked away from the table, sinking into a dark corner of the room, feeling too emotionally drained to even venture outside. He heard the colonel talking to an older woman, apparently a nurse.

"Katherine," he was saying wearily, "we're overwhelmed as it is now, and I'm afraid we have more coming. Six of my best doctors are now too ill with typhoid to work. I just sent them to bed." He rubbed his eyes, looking thoroughly exhausted and spent.

Katherine looked thoughtful. "I'll be right back," she said, and quickly left the bewildered colonel. She returned moments later with Amber in her wake.

"Colonel Duncan, this is Miss Amber Saxton. She's a foreigner and has been trained in medicine." She paused and lowered her voice. "She's a doctor."

The colonel raised his eyebrows and extended his hand to Amber. "And where is this miracle country, Miss Saxton?"

Amber smothered a yawn and cleared her throat. "It's a small island near South America. I doubt most people have ever heard of it."

"What's it called?" he pressed.

"Seattle," she replied smoothly, hoping the city hadn't yet been founded. Tyler watched her intently from the shadows.

"There's a mining town on the West Coast by that name," Duncan stated. "What a coincidence."

Tyler watched Amber squirm for a split second. "This is entirely different," she replied.

Colonel Duncan nodded. "Well, let me show you what we do in here." Tyler observed as the colonel showed Amber the medical equipment present and then moved on to describe many common wounds, using some of the soldiers present as examples. He explained that many of the soldiers had survived battlefield surgery and were sent to the hospital to recuperate before going home. Oftentimes the wounds worsened during the hospital stay, and patients often died or faced amputation. He stood back to watch as she began examining the soldiers on her own.

Amber nodded as she looked at the wounds, showing no signs of nausea or disgust. She spoke easily to the soldiers, asking them their names, where they were from, whether or not they had a wife or girl-friend back home. Tyler noticed many of the men attempting smiles for the first time since he'd entered the hospital.

One soldier seemed completely taken with her and lifted her hand into both of his own. He looked down at her finger and said, "What a pretty ring! Are you married, then?"

"No, I'm not married. This ring is my birthstone," she replied, trying to gently withdraw her hand. The soldier looked closely at it, squinting as though trying to read something small.

"What are these numbers for?" he asked her.

Tyler found himself holding his breath, wondering how she'd explain a year engraved on a ring over a century hence.

"Well, the numbers were put there in error," Amber explained quickly. "They're approximately two hundred years off. It should state 1792, the year my grandmother was born. She had the ring made just shortly before she passed away, but the jeweler made a mistake with the numbers." Amber laughed. "She decided to keep it just as it was. She had a wonderful sense of humor. The ring was given to me when she died because my birthstone is the same as hers was."

"And these letters, 'G.W.'," the soldier asked, "are they her initials?"

Amber swallowed. "Yes," she nodded. "Guenivere Williams. My maternal grandmother."

Katherine and Colonel Duncan were watching Amber, apprecia-tive of her natural ability with the wounded. Tyler did his best not to snort right out loud. Guenivere? If that really were her grandmother's name, he'd be surprised. *She lies well*, he thought with some relief and perhaps just a twinge of regret. He emerged from the shadows and approached her casually, wanting to be close at hand should she not continue to spin convincing stories.

"Oh. I didn't know you were here." Amber looked up in surprise.

"Do you two know each other?" Duncan asked Tyler.

"Well, we've never been properly introduced, but I believe we have Seattle in common," Tyler said, attempting a smile.

"You've been to Amber's home country?" Katherine asked, clearly interested.

"Oh, yes, many times." Tyler spoke pleasantly, warming to his tale. "It's an unforgettable little island; warm, lush, tropic. Why, it hardly ever rains and the sun shines all year." It wasn't often one was given an opportunity to dwell in the Twilight Zone. Might as well embellish the story a bit, he decided.

"It's quite lovely," Amber quickly agreed, looking at him with clearly written warning in her eyes.

"Well, my dear, that would account for your tanned skin," Katherine remarked and nodded to herself.

"Now, which port did you say you sailed into?" Colonel Duncan directed his question to Amber.

She cleared her throat and looked at Tyler in question, only to be met with a blank gaze and small shrug. She was saved from having to answer by a physician who approached Colonel Duncan with a question.

Amber took advantage of the fact that the colonel was distracted and closely observed the activity around her. She raised her eyebrows and shook her head slightly. "They're lucky they're not killing their patients with that ether," she said more to herself than Tyler.

"Why?"

"It's lethal in high doses," she explained. "They'd be better off doing this outside where the fresh air would make it a little less potent."

Her thoughts were interrupted by an abrupt noise from across the room. A wounded man was yelling incoherently and a doctor was call-ing for the colonel. Duncan and Katherine started for them, and Amber shook herself out of her musings to follow them. She stopped and turned to Tyler. "Quit spinning crazy stories about 'Seattle'!" she hissed. "What are you thinking?"

Tyler shrugged. "I'm keeping things interesting?"

Amber glared and followed the colonel and head nurse to the source of the disturbance.

"What's the problem, Matthews?" Duncan asked the surgeon.

"This man is delirious and we need to amputate his arm. He won't hold still long enough for us to administer the ether." Matthews was desperately trying to hold the man down. The poor soldier was thrashing wildly, trying to escape. "We still have quite a few men needing amputations and other attention—" the surgeon stopped talking as he was hit squarely in the side of the head by a flailing arm.

He recovered and punched the soldier in the face. The man slumped backward onto the table, unconscious. Amber smacked her palm against her forehead in disbelief, wishing she could transport the poor patient back home with her to a tidy, sterile operating room. She shot the physician a dark look as yet another doctor began the anesthetizing procedure with the ether and cloth.

"Who is this?" Matthews asked Duncan, scowling.

"Her name is Amber Saxton, and she claims to be a physician." The colonel was looking at Amber as though still questioning her authenticity.

"And you believe her?" the surgeon scoffed.

"She does have quite a way with the wounded," the colonel speculated.

"And I watched her in the patients' ward. She cleaned and rebandaged many ugly wounds." Katherine was defensive. She believed Amber's story wholeheartedly.

"So what? Any good nurse has 'a way' with the wounded and is handy with a bandage." Matthews was indignant. He glared at Amber. "Who do you think you are?"

"That's enough." The colonel interceded and turned toward Amber, who by this time was seething. "Have you ever done any amputating, Miss Saxton?"

"Yes, but I'm afraid our methods were a little different than yours seem to be." Amber warily eyed the amputating saw lying on the table.

Matthews grabbed the saw and said, "Well, stand back and learn then, Miss Doctor." Amber watched in horror as he lifted the saw and prepared to amputate.

"Wait!" she protested. "When was the last time you washed those filthy hands? And how about that . . . that instrument— has it been sterilized?"

Matthews looked at her in annoyance. "Listen. I don't have time to wash my hands every five minutes. This is a busy war. As for my trusty saw, allow me to demonstrate." He began the gruesome process, still speaking to her over his shoulder. "I am certain you can see that we are extremely busy tonight, so please excuse me while I do my job."

Amber lunged at him, only to be dragged off for the second time that day. "You don't know what you're doing!" she cried out in dismay. "You don't know the damage you're doing! He'll die from infection!"

Tyler pulled her firmly by the shoulders. "Come on, Dr. Saxton." He motioned apologetically to Katherine and the colonel. "I'll see her to her room." Meanwhile, Matthews finished his task. He wiped the saw on his bloody, filthy apron, held the menacing instrument in the air, and called out, "Next!"

Chapter 7

The rays of early morning sunlight spilled across Tyler's room and settled on his face. He hadn't rested well all night. Every time sleep had come to blissfully rescue his exhausted mind, he saw images of blood, dismembered limbs, and tortured faces. The gruesome pictures eventually gave way to a much more pleasant one—one with dark hair, forest-green eyes, a charming smile, and a small, well-toned frame.

He was struck with a sickening realization as he opened his eyes and viewed his surroundings. He wasn't home. He buried his face in his pillow and groaned. He remembered the conversation he'd had with an indignant Dr. Saxton the night before after he'd dragged her, protesting all the way, from the operating room.

"You don't understand," she'd said when he had managed to get her out of the building. "He's going to inadvertently kill that man!" Her eyes clouded over as she continued to struggle with Tyler.

"Hey, listen to me—*listen to me*!" He grabbed her shoulders and shook her, his face inches away from hers. "You can't just go barging in there telling them how to do their jobs! Do you honestly think they're going to listen to you? And what will you tell them, that you're from an advanced civilization years in the future?" He couldn't believe his own words.

His grip had lessened as she'd slumped her shoulders in defeat. Tears escaped her eyes and fell heedlessly down her cheeks. "I don't understand any of this. I just want to go home. But I can't be here and just watch as they make . . . *horrific* mistakes with human life."

Tyler viewed her dismay with something akin to sympathy. He wanted to cry himself. He swallowed past the unfamiliar lump in his throat and put an arm about her shoulders. "Come on. Let's get some sleep. Maybe we'll be home in the morning and I'll look you up in the phone book."

"My number's unlisted," she muttered, wiping at her eyes.

"Well, then, I'll find you at work. And we'll laugh at this whole stupid thing." He had reluctantly watched her walk into her own room across the hall from his and close the door. He felt as lonely and frightened as he had as a child.

The image of her face lingered in his mind as he awoke fully and rubbed his eyes. He moaned as he turned over, stiff from spending the night in a strange, uncomfortable bed. The quiet knock on the door drew him reluctantly into a sitting position.

"Come in," he groaned. The door opened and Boyd entered warily.

"Sir? Breakfast is in ten minutes," he announced. "Would you like me to wait outside the door for you?"

Tyler blinked. "Yes, Boyd. That would be fine. What time is it?"

"Nearly oh-six-hundred, sir."

Tyler swung his legs around and stood, stretching in an attempt to convince his aching body to respond. "You know, Boyd, you really don't have to call me 'Sir' all the time. My name is Tyler."

"Yes, sir."

Tyler quickly dressed and glanced at Amber's bedroom, which was empty, as he walked to breakfast with Boyd. He tried to shrug off his annoyance at the thought that she'd left the building without checking in with him first. His line of thinking rapidly changed its course as he considered the possibility that she'd been able to go "home" while he was still stuck in the odd time warp. His heart rate increased and he fought to maintain a calm façade as the blood roared in his ears. He stood in the food line next to Boyd, tray in hand, waiting for their food, which dangerously resembled dinner from the night before. Tyler groaned inwardly and sought a diversion from the nausea that threatened to engulf him.

He cleared his throat. "Boyd," he began, "have you seen Dr. Saxton this morning?" He hoped his voice didn't sound as desperate to the young man as it did to his own ears.

"The new nurse, you mean?" Boyd asked. "I know there's a nurse here by that name."

Tyler nodded. That's right, she was supposed to be a nurse. "Yes," he managed on a hoarse whisper. "Have you seen her today?"

Boyd nodded, much to Tyler's relief. "I saw her leaving the infirmary just as I knocked on your door this morning."

Tyler was disgusted at his reaction to the notion that he might have been left alone without a sympathetic ally. He was a self-made man who'd survived years of horrific treatment at the hands of one who should have loved him better than anyone. He found it particularly pathetic that he was relieved to the point of feeling faint that a certain doctor half his size and strength was still within easy reach.

He attempted to turn his mind to other matters. "So, tell me, Boyd. How is it that you're allowed to dine with the officers?"

Boyd awkwardly averted his gaze. "Uh, Colonel Duncan suggested you may need some help . . . adjusting."

Tyler gave a short, incredulous laugh. "You mean you're my chaperone?"

"I suppose so," Boyd mumbled uncomfortably.

"Well, I'll try to behave myself," Tyler said, doing his best to mask his sarcasm and spare the boy's feelings.

They progressed through the line and took their seats across from two doctors deep in conversation.

"I don't know," one doctor was saying. "I just find it odd, that's all. We've never had so much alcohol disappear at once."

The other doctor snorted. "I can think of plenty of wounded soldiers in there who would gladly help themselves to as much whiskey as they could get their hands on."

"Yes, but the cabinet hadn't been broken into," noted the first. "Whoever took it had a key."

"Were any of the men drunk or hung over this morning?" asked the second.

"No more so than usual," said the first. "None of the patients absolutely reeked of alcohol. I guess several men could have shared it all."

The doctors both shrugged and resumed eating. They all sat in silence until joined by a third doctor, one Tyler recognized from surgery the previous night. The physician nodded curtly and took a sip of his coffee. "I don't suppose any of you know the new nurse?" he asked sourly.

The doctor seated next to him turned his head and raised his eyebrows. "Which one?"

"The young one who thinks she's a doctor."

"Come to think of it, I did notice a pretty young thing in a nurse's uniform yesterday," the doctor leered.

"Yes, well, she may be pretty, but she's insane. She nearly attacked me yesterday while I was trying to amputate an arm," Matthews complained. "She was babbling on and on about washing my hands and the instruments."

The other doctor shrugged. "So, she's a neat nurse. It certainly wouldn't hurt to keep things clean around here."

Matthews rubbed his eyes. "It's not just that. I went in for my shift this morning, and all the surgical instruments smelled like whiskey. Whiskey! Can you imagine?"

The other two doctors exchanged glances. "Are you sure?"

Matthews looked annoyed. "Of course I'm sure. Someone 'bathed' the instruments in whiskey."

"And you think the new nurse is responsible?" ventured one.

"Well, who else would do such a stupid thing?" Matthews growled. "It's never happened before, has it?"

Tyler made an effort to suppress an irritated smile. Apparently she'd abandoned him *before* the rays of early morning sunlight had enveloped the earth. She apparently had not stayed in her bedroom the night before after he'd entered his. So much for her agreement to never leave him. She ought to at least have told him where she was going.

"Well, that would explain the empty whiskey bottles," offered one of the physicians.

Matthews raised his head. "What are you talking about?"

"Two of the large whiskey bottles were missing from the cabinet this morning." The doctor seated next to Matthews delivered the explanation, his mouth full.

Matthews exploded. "She used *our* whiskey? I refuse to tolerate this! She's wasting the only pain reliever we have available. I want her out of here!" He stomped off, leaving his breakfast on the table, untouched. The other doctors resumed their meals. Matthews was known for his hot temper and his self-inflated ego. Nobody ever paid too much attention to his ravings.

The doctor across from Tyler rolled his eyes. "He probably wanted the whiskey for himself."

Tyler nodded absently and rose, his intention to find Amber before the irate physician did, when he was intercepted by Colonel Duncan. "Captain." The colonel nodded and sat down on the bench. "It may be wise for you to review Major Andrews' old account books."

"Major Andrews?"

"The accountant you're replacing," Duncan explained.

"Oh, yes. Where can I find these books?"

"I have them," said Duncan. "Come to my office after breakfast and I'll give them to you."

"Fine. Thank you, sir." Tyler paused. "If I may ask, sir, why was Major Andrews here and not with his regiment?"

The colonel sighed. "Andrews was a personal friend of General Montgomery's. Montgomery made arrangements for Andrews to spend his last few days in a hospital instead of a tent. He was so ill from typhoid, his death was imminent."

Tyler nodded sympathetically, groaning inwardly. *Great*, he thought to himself as he dumped the contents of his tray and began his search for Amber. *If I'm here long enough, maybe I'll contract typhoid.*

****

Amber had been busy all morning. When she awoke, she had taken a quick peek into Tyler's room to assure herself she wasn't alone. He had been sleeping soundly, and she had envied the few moments of peace he was still enjoying. She had followed Katherine Hill from building to building as instructed, trying desperately to form the words to a prayer that might send her back home. All she could manage was a pathetic litany: *please, please, please.*

Just when she thought she'd surely go insane, she had been put to work cleaning and re-bandaging many seeping, festering wounds. *Ah,* she thought. *This I can handle.* Her mind was clear from that point onward; she convinced herself that she was doing nothing more than providing medical assistance for a remote, third-world country. Whenever reality threatened to overshadow her newfound sanity, she forced herself to focus on the patients at hand. She checked the progress of several unconscious patients, wishing fervently that she had her medical bag with all its wonderfully modern paraphernalia.

Her brows were presently knitted in a frown as she examined the side of a wounded soldier. The bullet had entered his body and had apparently been fished out by a hasty surgeon who, Amber supposed, had probably made the wound bigger during the extraction process. The resulting mess had been stitched sloppily and erratically. This poor boy had required a fairly elementary procedure and had obviously been improperly cared for.

She shook her head. "Who operated on this man?" she called over her shoulder to Katherine, who was attending the boy in the next bed.

"I did," came the masculine reply behind her. "What are you doing?"

Amber turned and flushed angrily as she recognized Matthews. "Wait one moment please," she gritted. "I'd like to talk to you."

Matthews snorted and folded his arms. "I'm not going anywhere."

Amber's hands flew as she fashioned two makeshift butterfly bandages to temporarily hold the sloppily sewn wounds more securely. Katherine looked on appreciatively, and by this time, several other doctors had wandered over to witness the confrontation between Matthews and his latest victim.

Amber helped the wounded soldier to get comfortable and smoothed his hair back from his damp forehead. "I'll be back soon," she murmured comfortingly. She turned and walked away from the soldier, motioning for Matthews to follow her. He was clearly annoyed at his lack of control with the woman. His fellow colleagues snickered, and he felt himself redden.

He followed Amber, his hands in fists and his expression menacing. "Just who do you think you are?" he demanded as he approached her. She had stepped from the infirmary and out into the crisp autumn air. They stood behind the building in an area secluded and hidden from view by several large bushes. "You have no place ordering me about and treating my patients!" He looked as though he wanted to strangle her, his face inches away from hers.

She made no attempt to back down or escape his outburst. She stood firm and glared at him, barely able to control her own fury. "You are the most incompetent physician I've ever seen in my life. That boy is a mess! You fished around with your fingers to find the bullet, didn't you." She didn't bother to phrase it as a question.

"Well, *doctor*," he sneered, "how would you suggest a bullet be removed?"

She ignored his comment. "And then you didn't even bother to stitch him up properly. How long did you plan to let him lie there and bleed?"

Matthews was indignant. "There were cases much more serious than his," he said defensively.

Amber couldn't help the fact that her jaw dropped in amazement. "So when were you going to see to him? Sometime today, after lunch?" She shook her head. "Do you have any idea how much blood he's lost? The nurses moved him and changed his bedding three times last night. Why they didn't notify anyone is completely beyond me."

"They didn't notify anyone on my orders! Bleeding is common for a wound of that sort." Matthews maintained his bravado, but took a small step backward.

"Common!" Amber's voice cracked. "It's hardly common if it's properly cared for as soon as the patient comes in!" She gritted her teeth and moved to step around Matthews. "I'm going to take care of this myself. Excuse me, doctor."

He quickly barred the entrance. "Don't you ever touch my patients!" he snarled. "I swear to you, lady, you'll regret it if you cross me!"

Amber willed her voice to stay calm. "You obviously don't know how to care for the man, so I'll do it. Otherwise, he's going to bleed to death."

"You're not even from this country!" the doctor shouted. "You don't know what you're doing, and aside from that, you're a woman!"

The comment found its mark. Amber's hands were clenched at her sides, her face displaying her utter disgust. "Let me tell you something. I'd match my skills as a second-year resident against yours any day. I've seen how you work, and let me tell you something else. If you were to practice medicine where I'm from the same way you do it here, you'd have a malpractice suit on your hands so fast your head would spin. Now get out of my way!"

The trembling in her voice matched the state of her body as her shoulders nearly shook with rage. The image of the incompetent physician's activities from the night before compounded her feelings tenfold, and she was surprised that her adrenaline hadn't impelled her to rip him from his spot in the doorway and throw him across the empty yard.

"I'm not moving." The comment was quiet and clipped. "I think you need to be taught a lesson." Had he simply raged at her, she might have anticipated his movement as he hit her across the face with the back of his hand. Her head snapped back in response, and as he raised his hand to repeat his actions, she tightened her fist and hit him in the throat as hard as she could. His eyes bulged as he choked, grabbing his neck with one hand and her throat with the other. She clutched his shoulders and thrust her knee upward into his groin. He crumpled to the ground in agony and grabbed for her skirt, just missing her as she rushed past him.

Tyler and Boyd were looking for Amber and happened upon the scene. Tyler stood with his mouth agape and slowly started to laugh. He was soon laughing so hard he was nearly doubled over. And to think he'd felt she would need his protection.

Boyd looked shocked. He opened his mouth to comment, only to close it again, unable to think of anything to say. He'd never seen a woman do that before.

****

Amber saw Tyler once in the afternoon, shortly after she'd experienced her confrontation with Matthews. They were surrounded by people and couldn't speak openly. "Mr. Montgomery," she'd said, smiling grimly. "How nice to see you here again today." He had nodded in response and murmured something about finding her later after he'd gone over some books.

She had motioned him close and hissed in his ear, "Don't tell any more wacky stories about balmy Seattle weather! I don't want to get caught up in your lies—I can't even keep my own straight!" She'd felt his eyes on her back as she moved on to her next task. *Well, let him be mad*, she thought. There was no way she was going to let him get his jollies at the risk of their safety.

As the day wore on, Amber kept busy attending the wounded, fixing mistakes, and helping wherever she could as the new wounded arrived. The air in the hospital carried a hopeless feeling of despair that seemed to settle upon everyone who worked with the soldiers. Most of the cases were so severe that there was little to do but watch the men die. Amber battled with her emotions as she observed the brave faces and the quiet demeanor of the patients, mostly young, who were approaching death. She was well aware of the fact that had she not been so concerned about returning home, she might have appreciated the hands-on experience of something most physicians only studied in history books.

She helped Katherine dole out supplies to the men who were well enough to return to their regiments: hats, scarves, mittens, socks—all donated by loving women and girls who wanted to express devotion and support to their men and their country.

Amber had to drag herself to dinner that night. She ached all over and was completely exhausted. She had slept very little the night before and had taken only fifteen minutes to gulp down her lunch. She was surprised that the day had passed uneventfully concerning Matthews. She had not seen or heard from him since she had rendered him helpless earlier that morning.

As she left the food line, she saw the colonel beckoning to her from an officer's table where he was sitting with Tyler and Boyd. He motioned for her to join them, and she gratefully sank down onto the hard wooden bench across from them.

"I am impressed, Dr. Saxton." Colonel Duncan smiled warmly at her. "Your skills as a physician are impeccable. How fortunate that you were raised in a country where your talents did not go to waste."

"Thank you, sir."

"I would very much like to visit this Seattle of yours," continued the colonel. "Perhaps when the war is over."

"Yes, perhaps." Amber stole a glance at Tyler, who smirked but remained silent. Amber continued addressing the colonel. "Sir, I must express my approval of your plans to avoid the spread of infection. The patient's ward is so desperately in need of a good, deep cleansing, and I offer my help in any way possible."

"Thank you. I accept your offer wholeheartedly," the colonel replied with a smile. "You should know firsthand from working all day what the conditions are like. We must start somewhere. I'm afraid I'm among only a handful of doctors who feel such action is necessary. Perhaps with time, the ideas will spread."

"I'm sure they will." Amber offered a small, thoughtful smile and reflected on the sterile environment in which she was accustomed to working.

The group had eaten in companionable silence for several minutes when a private approached the colonel and saluted. "Sir, a messenger from the Pennsylvania Seventh Infantry has just delivered this and said it should go directly to you." The colonel took the envelope and dismissed the boy.

He withdrew a piece of paper and read it twice, his expression grim. He set it on the table and looked up at Amber. "I'm afraid this concerns you, Miss Saxton."

She attempted a small laugh. "I've been here for only two days. What could possibly concern me?"

"Why don't you read this yourself." He handed her the letter.

October 18, 1862

Colonel Duncan:

It has come to my attention that several of our U.S. Army regiments are in dire need of qualified, competent medical personnel.

There are not nearly enough doctors and nurses available to attend the wounded on the battlefield.

I am currently visiting the camp of the Pennsylvania Seventh, now stationed ten miles to the north of your position. I am unable to leave at the moment, so I send you this most urgent request by way of messenger in hopes that you will agree with my opinions. I have just met a sergeant who left your hospital this morning. He had been treated by a foreign doctor, a Miss Amber Saxton. He described his wound to me and showed me how he had been treated by Dr. Saxton. This regiment is badly in need of medical personnel, and I am convinced that her services would be an asset. I understand from the sergeant that Miss Saxton is officially recognized as a nurse, and therefore she is under my jurisdiction. It is my wish that Dr. Saxton join the regiment and render her services on their behalf.

Enclosed, please find Dr. Saxton's transfer orders, signed by myself and a representative from the Health Commission.

Thank you.
Dorothea Dix

Amber looked up slowly. "This seems a bit odd. Is this a common request?"

Colonel Duncan was thoughtful for a moment. "I know Miss Dix quite well. She has requested transfers before, but only from hospital to hospital, never to a traveling regiment. The nurses assisting the surgeons at the battle sites usually come out locally or travel with them on a voluntary basis."

"Where's the transfer order that was mentioned in the letter?"

Duncan pulled another piece of paper from the envelope and unfolded it, inspecting it closely. "It certainly looks authentic. This is her signature." He handed it to Amber.

She read it and shrugged wearily. "I guess I have no choice." She had not even had a chance to get used to her routine at the hospital. She wasn't thrilled at the prospect of going into battle. She glanced at Tyler, suddenly struck by the realization that they'd be separated.

The colonel seemed perplexed. "There's something I haven't understood from the beginning about your presence here, Miss Saxton. Perhaps you can answer some questions for me."

Amber swallowed and tore her gaze away from Tyler, who was watching her intently. "What would you like to know, Colonel?"

"You have, apparently, never met Dorothea Dix," he stated.

She paused. "No, sir."

"I must admit, I find this confusing," he said. "Miss Dix is the only one in the position to hire Army nurses. She interviews all the candidates and has sole authority to accept or reject each applicant. Who, exactly, hired you?"

"Actually, sir, no one really did. I sort of wormed my way in." She smiled weakly.

"I assume Miss Hill must have taken a liking to you and decided to overlook the fact that you'd never been officially hired," he guessed.

"Please don't blame Katherine," said Amber. "This whole affair is really not her doing, believe me."

"Well, you have certainly proven yourself capable, and at any rate, it seems you now have Miss Dix's formal approval," said the colonel. "It's official. You are now employed with the United States Army."

"This is truly not a day I ever expected to see in my life."

"You'll leave the hospital tomorrow with Captain Montgomery, here," the colonel added. "He's joining that particular regiment as well, so you can travel together."

Amber breathed an inward sigh of relief. She hadn't been sure how she'd smuggle a two-hundred-pound man across the country on horseback. She only knew she wouldn't leave without him. The notion was unthinkable.

****

Hiding in the shadows of a dark corner, Matthews observed the small party at the officer's table. He rubbed his bruised throat and scowled. Although he would have liked to exact revenge on the girl with his own two hands, he had to smile at his cleverness. The forgeries had been simple, the letter believable, and he watched through narrowed eyes as Amber read her transfer order a third time.

He caught the young messenger outside the tent and handed him an urgent message to be taken immediately to General Montgomery. Its contents included a letter from Miss Dix that offered the services of one very qualified Dr. Saxton and instructions that she be required to travel with the regiment and serve with its medical team. Let the muskets have her, he thought to himself. With any luck, if he ever did see her again, she'd look much like the wounded she'd been working on all day.

Chapter 8

Amber shivered as cold drops of rain splashed against her face. She tugged the old wool cape more firmly about her shoulders and shoved her hair back underneath the large hood. She longed for her warm, down-filled coat hanging in the closet at the apartment she shared with Camille.

The sky was dark and the rain merely a prelude to the harsh winter snows which would soon cover the earth like a massive blanket. Amber shifted in the uncomfortable saddle and wished for the hundredth time she was in a heated car. Even the old Volkswagen bug she had driven in high school would have been better than riding ten miles on horseback.

She glanced over at Tyler, who sat comfortably on his mount. They followed Boyd, who was also on horseback. "Of course you would know how to ride a horse," she said to Tyler, annoyed. "Are you ever not in control of your life?"

"At this moment my life is approximately 137 years off," Tyler replied dryly. "I'd say I am definitely not in control."

She shook her head. "That's not what I mean. You seem like you actually fit in here. People are always looking at me like I've lost my mind. You must be one of those people who's led a completely charmed life—you know, always in possession of the perpetual horseshoe."

He turned mocking eyes on her. "My life has been anything but charmed, so you can stop feeling sorry for yourself."

Amber raised her eyebrows. "Excuse me, you poor, sensitive thing. Did we wake up on the wrong side of the bed this morning?"

Tyler shot her an irritated glance. "I woke up in the wrong bed, period."

Amber snorted. "Probably not the first time that's happened," she muttered under her breath.

Tyler raised one eyebrow and stared at her for so long that her face warmed under his gaze. He opened his mouth to say something, but apparently thought better of it. "I think I'll ride up here where the company's a little more pleasant," he finally said with a barely perceptible smirk, and pulled forward alongside Boyd, leaving Amber to ride by herself.

"Fine," Amber shot back. "And might I add that the company back *here* has just improved immeasurably!" She justified her snide remark about his "sleeping" habits by telling herself she would never have been rude if he hadn't started the whole thing by snapping at her. She did her best to hide her annoyance and said nothing for the remainder of the ride. They reached camp as the light was beginning to fade. The sight before them was a dreary one. The regiment had set up camp on a barren-looking field. There were tents spaced approximately three feet apart and hundreds of men were milling around, preparing for dinner and trying to stay warm.

Amber stared at the scene before them with her eyes wide. "This is unbelievable," she murmured. "It's like a Hollywood set."

Boyd glanced at her questioningly.

Tyler reined his horse in next to Amber and leaned over near her ear. "That's why people think you're an idiot," he said quietly.

Amber glared at him and attempted to gracefully dismount. Her legs and feet were numb with cold, which made the process increasingly difficult. She slipped and fell with her left foot still in the stirrup. She grimaced as mud splashed up into her face and oozed between her fingers where she had planted her hands in an attempt to soften the fall.

Tyler sat on his horse and rolled his eyes heavenward as Boyd scrambled around and tried to lift Amber from behind. He was able to hold her steady while she fumbled with the stirrup, which still held her bound. She finally freed her foot and took a step backward, only to lose her balance again, this time taking Boyd down with her as she fell.

"Oh, Boyd, I'm so sorry!" Amber scrambled in the mud, trying desperately to stand. She glared at Tyler, who was making no attempt to hide his mirth. "You shut up!" she snapped in annoyance. "If you're not willing to help, then stay out of it."

Boyd's face reddened considerably as he stood and attempted to wipe the mud from the seat of his pants. "Are you all right, ma'am?"

"Yes, thank you. I'm fine," she answered, struggling for a modicum of dignity.

"I'll help you find the general and get settled, and then I'll be riding back to the hospital," Boyd said.

"But Boyd, it's getting dark and it will rain soon. Don't you want to camp here for the night?"

"Thank you, ma'am, but I'll be fine," Boyd replied. "The pace going back will be much faster. I'll get a fresh horse and . . ."

They were interrupted by a gruff voice. "What's going on up here?"

Tyler twisted in his saddle and observed the man who was approaching their small party. Boyd immediately stiffened and saluted when he saw the emblems on the man's uniform, signifying his rank as general. Tyler dismounted and saluted as well. Amber hesitantly raised her hand to her brow, awkward with the unfamiliar motion.

Tyler stared as the man drew close. He had occasionally reflected on the comments that Colonel Duncan had made to him during their first encounter about the fact that Tyler's name was the same as the general's. He had realized that he would eventually meet one of his own ancestors. Nothing, however, could have prepared him for the shock of actually seeing the man face to face.

His own resemblance to the general was unmistakable. With a sudden swiftness, he remembered Stuart Tyler Montgomery IV, his grandfather, telling him when he was a young boy about the very first Stuart Tyler Montgomery who had been a Union Army general in the Civil War. "Wear the name proudly, son," his grandfather had said. "You come from a long line of noble men."

The words echoed in his mind as he stared at the man now standing before him. A long line of noble men, excluding his own father, Tyler had firmly decided long ago. He blinked as Stuart Tyler Montgomery the first shouted in his face, "Answer me, Captain!"

The general looked very annoyed. Amber quickly moved to Tyler's side and laid her hand softly on the general's arm. "Forgive him, sir," she murmured in a sweet, soothing voice. "This is Captain James T. Kirk. He has recently been in an accident which dulled his senses, making his reactions rather slow." She turned deliberately to Tyler. "Captain, I believe we are in the presence of the great General Montgomery."

"Just what I need," muttered the general. "A slow accountant."

"Oh, sir, I assure you, his skills as an accountant have not been impaired," Amber hastily interjected.

The general looked at Amber as though seeing her for the first time. His expression changed as he examined her more closely. "And who might you be?"

She lowered her lashes effectively. "I am Amber Alexandra Saxton, sir." She paused. "I have my transfer orders here from Dorothea Dix. I'm a physician."

"Ah, yes. Dr. Saxton," he said. "I had expected you, however, to be a man."

Before he could continue, Amber distracted him by serenely launching into her story about the lush, tropical island of Seattle.

Tyler stared at her. Demure she was *not*. He could not possibly be looking at the same woman he had seen in action at the Army hospital. She had clearly missed her calling in life. She deserved an Academy Award.

"Apparently Miss Dix felt my services with your regiment would be appreciated," she was saying.

"Most assuredly, yes," the general agreed. "You'll make a beautiful addition to our little family."

Amber smiled softly and laid a hand on her chest. "Oh, sir, you flatter me."

The general drew her arm within his own and began walking toward the camp. He took in her disheveled and muddy appearance. "Come with me, Miss Saxton, and we'll find a place for you to freshen up before dinner."

"Why, thank you, sir," she purred. "I'm honored that you should accompany me personally."

"Captain!" he barked over his shoulder to Tyler. "Bring Miss Saxton's things and follow us."

Tyler shook himself out of his daze and grabbed the reins of

Amber's horse as well as those of his own. "I suppose I'm now her personal valet," he muttered to himself.

Boyd caught Tyler's arm and said, "I'll just head back now, Captain. I can see that you'll be fine, and I wish you the best of luck."

Tyler switched the horses' reins to one hand and offered the other to Boyd, surprised by the pang of regret he felt at parting. "I can't thank you enough, Boyd, for all your help. Take care of yourself."

"Yes, sir. You do the same." He paused. "Will you bid my farewells to Dr. Saxton, please? I don't want to interrupt her now. Why don't you let me see to the horses."

"Thank you, Boyd." Tyler removed his and Amber's belongings from the saddles. "I'll tell Amber you said good-bye." Tyler watched as Boyd moved toward camp with the horses. Amber had worried needlessly, he realized as Boyd disappeared from view. The boy had a good head on his shoulders and would reach his destination in no time.

The general, meanwhile, had paused to speak with a passing lieutenant, but held Amber's arm firmly within his own. Outwardly she appeared docile and acquiescent. Inwardly she was uncomfortable. She threw Tyler a dark look over her shoulder as he approached with their bags, and she mouthed the words, "You owe me one!" He merely scowled in return.

She certainly didn't object to being treated nicely. And despite the fact that she was a definitive product of late twentieth-century society, she held the view that chivalry was a good thing and regretted its general loss. It was the general's probing gaze and patronizing demeanor that bothered her. She couldn't imagine having to act as though the only thoughts in her head were concerns about social graces. In the course of her young life she had felt the barbs of chauvinism, comments made by people who didn't know better, but should have. She realized that her present situation would be worse than anything she had encountered in her own century. Matthews' reaction to her should have been her first indication that she was facing an uphill climb. She had dismissed his attitude as singular, not wanting to acknowledge that she was now immersed in a time period when women were not even allowed to vote.

The general led them to a small tent and barked at Tyler to help her get comfortable. "I would stay and assist you myself," he said to

Amber, "but unfortunately I have other pressing business needing my attention."

"Of course, sir. I understand," she said with a smile.

He bent and kissed her hand. Before she could recover from her surprise, he turned and was gone. Tyler shifted the bags he carried and, brushing past her, entered the tent. She quickly followed to escape the sharp blast of wind that penetrated her heavy cloak.

The tent offered paltry shelter from the elements, and while it was notably larger than those that surrounded it, it was barely tall enough for Tyler to stand upright inside. He unceremoniously dumped her bag on the only item of furniture within, a small cot, and turned to face her. "What do you call that scene back there?" he demanded.

Amber removed her hood and ran a hand through her disheveled hair in an attempt to return some semblance of order to her appearance. "I call it saving your sorry hide," she retorted. "It was obvious that we were standing face to face with someone from your family tree, and might I add that the apples surely don't fall far from it. You look just like the man."

He shook his head. "So you decided that because I look like him, I must be related?"

"No," she snapped. "If you'll recall, you told me when we first met that your grandfather five generations back was a general. When I saw this man, I came to the same conclusions you obviously did. Now am I right?"

Tyler rubbed his eyes. "Yes, I suppose so. My full name is Stuart Tyler Montgomery the sixth." He looked at Amber. "What did you tell him my name was?"

"Captain James T. Kirk," she laughed. "I hope you're a Star Trek fan."

"I'm not. I should kill you for that alone." His expression was little short of menacing.

"Well, can you imagine trying to explain to the man the reason your name is exactly the same as his?"

"I suppose I should thank you for thinking so quickly."

"I wasn't expecting you to. You're about as cordial today as a shark," she fired back.

"When I woke up at the hospital the very first time, I was in shock," he muttered. "Now I'm just mad."

"Well, don't take it out on me—I'm not exactly thrilled to be here, either," Amber responded. "All I can say is I hope we're not going to be here long. If the decline in your mood is any indication of how it's going to be from here on out, you'll be a maniac by the time we get home."

He smirked. "Are you offended because I don't fall at your feet the way all the other lovesick soldiers do?"

She smiled good-naturedly and removed her wet cloak. "They're not lovesick. They just welcome a friendly feminine face." Her expression changed. "I must say, though, I think your ancestor's a bit perverted. He's old enough to be my father, and he . . ." She trailed off, brushing the thought aside.

Tyler narrowed his eyes. "He what?"

Amber frowned slightly. "He made me uncomfortable. It was the way he leered, I guess. He was too forward—he invaded my space."

"Well, I must say, you certainly play the part of the stupid female very well," Tyler noted.

"I did that for your sake, 'Captain!'" Amber fumed. "You were so shocked at seeing an image of yourself thirty years from now that you couldn't even tell the man your name!"

"Well, I hope I'm around to see you encounter one of *your* dead ancestors," he said.

Amber began pulling clothing out of her bag. "Actually, I did have one way back who fought during the Civil War. He was the only male survivor in his family. That's all I know about him, though. His name was Weldon Saxton." She glanced at Tyler. "I guess I'll keep an eye out for him." She pulled her wrinkled green surgery scrub suit from the bag and dumped it on the cot.

Tyler picked it up and laughed. "Is this what you were wearing when you got here?"

"Yes. Poor Katherine thought I was from another planet," she said. "What were you wearing?"

"A shirt and tie. Armani slacks."

Amber looked at him and laughed as he described Duncan's reaction at their initial meeting. *Her eyes light up when she smiles*, thought Tyler. Then he mentally shook himself, as he always did when he found himself getting too comfortable with another person—especially a woman. Noncommittal sex was one thing. Emotional attachment was an entirely different matter. With so much currently at stake, he couldn't afford to muddle his thinking. It had never been a problem before; there was no reason it should suddenly become an issue.

He walked abruptly to the tent flap. "I'm going to check out the camp. I'll be back in a while." He was gone before she could even blink. She stared for a moment at the spot he had just vacated and shook her head. He was definitely too complex to analyze. Awfully nice to look at, though.

The tent suddenly felt extremely empty. She fought an insane impulse to dash out of the tent, find Tyler and grab onto his hand as though it were a lifeline. She looked around the tent and felt a stab of panic. *What am I doing here?!* The thought had repeated itself so many times during the past forty-eight hours that she felt she would surely go mad.

She had never questioned her relationship with her Heavenly Father. Her testimony of the gospel of Jesus Christ was second nature to her; spirituality had been a relatively easy and uncomplicated part of her life. She often prayed throughout her workday, making requests to her Heavenly Father that she might be blessed to remember all she'd learned and be able to do her job well. She prayed regularly each night before bed as well; sometimes "before bed" meant 6:00 a.m. after coming home from work, but she always made an effort to express her wishes and gratitude.

I guess I haven't been grateful enough, she thought as she looked around the cramped tent. *There's something to be said for avoiding complacency and an excessive amount of arrogance. Look at what can happen.*

She sat slowly on her cot with a sudden realization that when she was a child, she had viewed the medical profession with a certain awe and reverence. But since achieving her goals in early adulthood, she had neglected to acknowledge that her amazing academic and medical talents were a blessing. She had done so well for so long that she had become accustomed to believing that there wasn't a thing on earth she couldn't accomplish. And truth be told, she realized, she probably could have accomplished just about anything, so great was her determination. But in allowing herself to forget that her talents were heaven-sent, she'd done herself a disservice. Humility was a quality she'd not possessed for a long time.

Well, this is quite the reminder. She looked around the small tent again in despair. She fought to keep her breathing regular and deep, and closed her eyes. *I will get through this,* she resolved, and clenched her jaw. *I will get through this and I will go home. And what a story I'll have when I get there.*

Chapter 9

Amber dressed as warmly as she could. She donned the thermal underwear she had been wearing under her scrub suit the day she arrived at the Army hospital, and put on her only other nurse's uniform. Thankfully, it was black and made of heavy material that provided some warmth. Amber was eternally grateful that Dorothea Dix was a practical woman who didn't dress her nurses in ruffled pinafores and thin material. She had exchanged her tight women's boots for a smaller pair of men's combat boots she'd found in the supply room. She didn't care who stared. She was not going to march in shoes that one of her childhood dolls could have comfortably worn.

When she was so hungry she could no longer stand it, she put on her woolen cloak and stepped outside to brave the elements. The rain had stopped, but the air was still cold and the heavy clouds threatened to resume their tirade.

Men in blue uniforms were milling around everywhere, and when she failed to spot Tyler, she followed the direction most of the men seemed to be taking. She soon found herself staring at a long line of soldiers who were waiting patiently to enter a tent, which was obviously being used as a mess hall. She sighed inwardly and headed for the end of the line, which seemed to stretch for miles, when she was stopped by a firm hand on her elbow. "Miss Saxton?"

She turned and found herself staring into the bluest eyes she'd ever seen. "Yes?"

"General Montgomery sent me to find you. He would like you to join him for dinner in his tent." The man smiled, revealing a row of even, white teeth.

Amber hesitated, then nodded and smiled. She and Tyler would be much better off if she remained on good terms with the general. She didn't know where Tyler had gone, but decided with a small amount of spite that he could fend for himself. He hadn't bothered to show his face for well over an hour. "Thank you very much, sir," she said.

The man touched the brim of his hat and nodded to her. "Major O'Brian at your service, Miss. Please, call me Ian."

Amber allowed him to guide her away from the food line toward a large tent approximately twenty yards off. They reached the opening and Major O'Brian entered and pulled her in behind him, his broad shoulders temporarily obstructing her view of the tent's occupants. He cleared his throat and the general looked up from his meal. Amber steeled herself and stepped out from behind her human shield.

"Ah, Miss Saxton," the general remarked, rising and extending his hand. "It's good of you to join us." He pulled her arm through his own when she reached his side and turned her toward the other men seated at the table. "Allow me to introduce you to these men."

He began rattling off the names and ranks of the seven men, and they each nodded as they were introduced. He ended with, "And you already know Captain Kirk, our new accountant." He winked at Amber and said to her confidentially, "You were right, my dear. His accident did not in the least impair his skills as an accountant. He'll do just fine."

Amber smiled and replied, "I'm glad his talents are adequate enough to allow him to serve under such a man as yourself." She glanced over at Tyler to see him rolling his eyes at her obvious attempt to flatter the man. The effort on her part to withhold a snarl was tremendous; who did he think he was, taking off and finding dinner for himself while she had been wandering the camp, wondering if there would be any food left by the time she made it through the long line at the mess tent? Her eyes narrowed a fraction, her irritation fueled by a stabbing hunger pain in the pit of her stomach, and she forced her attention on the general, who was still speaking.

Montgomery addressed the men at the table. "Gentlemen," he said, "this little beauty is Miss Amber Saxton. She's joining our medical team at the recommendation of Dorothea Dix." The general patted Amber's hand as though she was a child and said to the men, "She claims to be a doctor."

The men tried to hide their smiles. Some coughed, others quickly shoved food in their mouths. The general continued, "I'm sure Dr. Davis can put her to work. There are plenty of bandages that need folding and instruments to be organized." He turned to Amber with a smile. "Are you ready to eat, my dear?" He led her to a chair opposite Tyler and next to his own. She sat in it, dumbfounded. *Well, Amber, you wanted humility, you got it.*

Tyler glanced at her, surprised that she apparently wasn't going to defend herself. He'd fully expected her to, and had been trying to decide how to soften her remarks after she'd fired them off. When she made no attempt to say anything, he felt the familiar stirrings that always struck when he witnessed the plight of the downtrodden. He attempted to shove the urges out of his mind, but he realized he was fighting a losing battle when he saw that Amber was too incredulous to even eat. That particular fact spoke volumes; he knew she was probably starving.

"I've seen Dr. Saxton perform surgery on wounded men," he said casually, raising his fork to his mouth. The other men stared at him. "She's very effective. I watched her operate at the hospital just yesterday."

Amber's head snapped up and she looked at him in shock. The general slowly chuckled. "Son, your brain has truly suffered from that blow to the head. We're talking about a woman."

Oh, enough already! Amber had reached her limit and opened her mouth to reply, only to be smoothly cut off by Tyler. His voice carried an undercurrent of warning as he addressed the general. "Dr. Saxton is a competent physician. She's more than competent. If she's saving the lives of your wounded soldiers, why does it matter that she's a woman?"

The general narrowed his eyes and glared at Tyler. "I'll not have a woman performing surgery on my men. She can see to their needs in the capacity of a nurse. I have my reservations about her traveling with the regiment in the first place. If you'll notice, there are no other women in camp because I don't allow it." He took a deep breath. "I've decided to allow her to stay with us because it interests me to do so. This discussion is closed."

Amber desperately wanted to say something on her own behalf. She looked at Tyler, who discreetly shook his head as if reading her thoughts. She fumed in frustration and ate her meal in silence. The conversation at the table resumed as if she were no longer there.

When the meal was finished, the men were dismissed and Amber rose from the table. The general stopped her from leaving. "I'd love the pleasure of your company for a while, Miss Saxton." She nodded her consent, which he allowed her to do as a mere formality, and he turned to Tyler. "Captain, return in one hour to escort Miss Saxton to her tent."

The general was interrupted as Major O'Brian entered the tent with a folded paper in his hand. Montgomery quickly scanned the contents and replied, "Is the messenger waiting?"

"Yes, sir," O'Brian replied.

The general turned to Amber. "I'm sorry about this delay. I'll return shortly." He glanced at Tyler on his way out. "You're dismissed," he snapped.

Major O'Brian advanced toward Amber as the general exited the tent. He bowed and kissed her hand. "Miss Saxton," he murmured, smiling.

Amber was amused. These men had obviously not seen women in a long time. "Hello, Ian," she replied.

Tyler raised his eyebrows at Amber. "Making friends already, Doctor?"

Ian glanced at Tyler and turned back to Amber. "May I escort you to your tent?"

"Dr. Saxton is visiting with the general for an hour, and then *I* will be escorting her to her tent," Tyler firmly interceded.

Ian looked annoyed. "Perhaps another time," he smiled at Amber. He cast another glance over his shoulder at Tyler and left.

"You're getting awfully protective, Captain Kirk," Amber remarked with a smile.

Tyler scowled. "I don't trust anyone here. We have to blend in as well as possible." He lowered his voice. "We're in trouble if they find out I'm not really a captain in the Army and there's not really an island off the coast of South America called Seattle—we'd be hanged as spies. I forged my identification papers with my lovely new name," he glared, "but I'm hoping nobody examines them too carefully."

He moved closer to Amber. "You need to remember to keep your temper. For some strange reason, the general has taken a liking to you."

"Why is that so strange?" Amber demanded with a mixture of amusement and annoyance.

Tyler ran a hand through his hair. "You know what I mean. Just keep him pacified. Don't blare your trumpet for gender equality or try to prove your intelligence to him." He paused and looked intently at Amber. "If he touches you, if you feel threatened in any way, you scream. I won't be very far away."

Amber tried to shrug off his serious tone. She smiled. "I'll be fine. Don't worry about me. I've dealt with troublesome men before."

"Not like this, I'm sure. I don't like him." Tyler's face tensed, and he clenched and unclenched his fist. *He's just like my father.*

Before Amber could reply, the general reentered the tent and glared at Tyler. "I told you to leave," he said. Tyler merely saluted, glanced briefly at Amber, and left.

"He worries about me, you know. I think he's adopted me as his little sister," Amber offered in explanation.

"Of course." General Montgomery pulled aside a chair for Amber and motioned for her to sit. "So my dear, tell me all about yourself."

Chapter 10

"So, what did you tell him?" Tyler prodded her as they walked back to her tent.

"I'll get to that in a minute," Amber responded. "What I'd like to know is why you decided to join the general for dinner without so much as a word to me about it. I had no idea where I was going, and . . ."

Tyler scowled. "The general snagged me while I was out looking around and basically ordered me to join him. He said he'd send someone to get you and wouldn't let me leave. Now what did you tell him?"

Amber sighed. "He asked me about myself, and I was as honest as I dared be. I figure, the fewer lies I tell, the less I'll have to remember." She gave him a sidelong glance. "And don't worry. I managed to control my temper and maintain an appropriate and genteel feminine exterior." She smirked. "I think he likes me even more now than he did before."

Tyler's expression was grim. "I assumed you'd be pleased," she said, surprised. "As long as I can keep him happy, we may just make it home intact."

He shook his head. "Just be careful when you're alone with him." They reached the entrance to her tent.

"Why are you so suspicious of him? Do you know something I don't?" she questioned.

He looked directly into her face. "I'm the only one around here who can even remotely begin to understand where you come from and why you think the way you do," he said quietly. "These people are not at all concerned about being politically correct. Just watch what you say, especially to the general. Believe me when I say that I don't trust him, and I'm sure that before this whole ordeal is finished I will be embarrassed to be related to him."

She raised her eyebrows. "I suppose I'll have to trust your judgment." She moved to enter her tent and turned back as an afterthought. "You know, I realize there aren't going to be too many people here who will believe I'm a physician. I just want you to know that I appreciate the way you defended me tonight at dinner. It was actually kind of nice. I'm used to fighting my own battles." She laughed. "And to think you told me not to lose my temper!"

"I didn't lose my temper."

"No, but you certainly weren't too concerned about 'keeping the general pacified'," Amber smirked.

"I can take care of myself with my grandfather."

"But I can't?"

"No," Tyler said flatly.

"Why not?" she questioned, the corner of her mouth quirked into a half-smile.

He shook his head. "Look at you! You could never hold your own if he were to get violent with you."

Amber laughed. "Why are you automatically assuming he's violent? He's chauvinistic and patronizing, yes, but—"

"He's also ignorant, prejudiced, and mean," Tyler returned. "Just watch your step."

She sighed and decided to change the subject. "So, now that I've been officially escorted back to my tent, what am I supposed to do? I have no lamp, no candle, certainly no flashlight and nothing to read. I can't write home because I have nothing to write with or on, and at any rate, my parents haven't been born yet." She smiled. "I suppose my options are fairly limited."

"There's a camp full of men who would love to entertain you, I'm sure," he remarked dryly.

She laughed softly. "I think I'd rather read."

"What do you like to read?"

"At this point, I'd read anything I could get my hands on," Amber said with a yawn.

"Well, maybe we should just try to get some sleep. It's getting late. My tent isn't far from yours." He pointed to a tent approximately ten yards off.

Amber stifled the urge to beg him to remain with her. *You're a big girl, Amber. You can sleep in a tent by yourself.* She reluctantly nodded. "Well, good night then. I guess I'll see you in the morning."

"Probably, if our luck doesn't change." He made sure she was safely inside her tent before he left.

Amber tried to amuse herself by draping her wet clothing around the tent and organizing the few personal articles Katherine had given her. She kept herself busy for approximately thirty minutes when she realized that there was absolutely nothing left for her to do. She sat down on her cot and cupped her chin in her hands, thoroughly agitated and restless. Though tired, she was hours away from sleep and knew that to attempt it would be futile, so she decided to venture outside again and look for the medical station. She was pulling her cloak tight about her shoulders when she heard movement outside her tent flap.

"Amber?" She jumped at the voice. "Are you asleep?"

She moved to the tent opening and peered out. "Tyler?" He stood before her with a small lantern and a book. "Come in here," she beckoned as the icy rain began to fall in large drops. The tent blocked out most of the wind and was dry, at least.

He stepped inside and set the lamp on the ground. "Compliments of the general. I'm sure we'll find him very accommodating when it comes to your needs. I mentioned you could use a lantern and he had men jumping left and right to fulfill your wishes."

Amber motioned for him to sit next to her on the cot. "What's that?" she asked as he tried to make himself comfortable in the small confines of the tent. He handed her a small, black book.

"I'm not sure, exactly. It looks like a weird Bible. It comes to you with love from your friend, Major O'Brian," Tyler drawled out the last. He watched as Amber held the book tenderly, almost reverently, her eyes wide. "What's wrong?"

"It's a Book of Mormon." She shook her head in disbelief and gently turned the pages. "Wow," she whispered. "It's in paragraph form." She looked up at Tyler. "Where did you say this came from?"

"Major O'Brian."

"So Ian is a Mormon?"

Tyler shrugged. "I don't know. Why, are you?"

"Yes." She turned her attention back to the book. Tyler studied her closely, looking perplexed. She glanced up and gave him a wry smile. "Are you looking for horns? Or maybe you're wondering how many wives my father has."

"Actually, I was wondering if you drink—and whether or not you've ever slept with anyone."

Amber met his gaze and wanted desperately to wipe the arrogant smirk from his face. She smiled. "Is that all you know about my religion? That we don't believe in premarital sex or drinking?"

"No, I know a little more." He shifted on the cot, and Amber wondered if she had imagined the flash of irritation in his eyes that dissipated as quickly as it had come. He interrupted her thoughts with one eyebrow raised. "I suppose you have a working knowledge of all major world religions."

"As a matter of fact, yes. What would you like to know?"

"What can you tell me?"

"How much time do you have?" she questioned with a grin.

"All the time in the world, apparently."

Amber launched into a brief synopsis of several major Middle and Far Eastern religions, then addressed the fundamental Christian religions of the Western world and ended with the basic gospel principles of the LDS faith. Tyler merely studied her face, saying nothing. She closed her ten-minute soliloquy with a smile. "I wanted to make an educated choice."

"I see. And your studies led you to Mormonism."

"Something like that. Actually, I was there all along. I was raised a Latter-day Saint."

He regarded her intently, making her feel slightly uncomfortable. "You know, you never did answer my original question."

"You didn't phrase it in the form of a question," Amber retorted. "And it's none of your business anyway."

"What are you ashamed of?"

Amber's eyebrows drew together in a bemused frown. "I'm surprised at your audacity. You really are lacking in interpersonal skills, you know. Are you always so blunt?"

He leaned forward and rested his elbows on his knees. His eyes were serious. "The only reason I ever ask questions of people is to get information I feel I might need. With women I usually use charm and flattery, but I get the feeling that won't be effective or necessary with you."

"So what kind of information about me do you feel you might be needing? I can tell you this much—I don't think the status of my virginity has any bearing on our current . . . predicament." She was torn between amusement and irritation.

"Actually, I just wanted to satisfy my own curiosity on that point." His mocking smile was fleeting and quickly faded. He sighed and sat back, running a hand through his hair. "As much as it pains me to admit this, I think we're stuck here for a while. I have no idea why, and I don't know what we're supposed to be doing. I'd be much more comfortable having just myself to take care of—"

She cut him off. "You really think you need to take care of me?" She shook her head in disbelief. She wasn't offended, just surprised. No one had felt responsible for her since she had lived at home with her parents. She'd been taking care of herself for so long that Tyler's implication caught her off guard. "I suppose I should be flattered, but then, you've decided not to use flattery on me, haven't you?"

He rolled his eyes at her. "Look, all I'm saying is that I would like to get back to my life, and I'm sure you'd like to do the same. I don't know anything about you and I don't want you doing or saying anything that will put us at more of a risk than we're already facing. Your flimsy excuse of being a foreigner is going to hide your odd behavior for only so long. You have got to stop blurting out every little thing that crosses your mind."

Amber smiled, her eyes narrowing. "Contrary to what you may believe, *Captain Kirk*," she replied, placing deliberate emphasis on the name she had fabricated for him, "I am a bright woman. I don't need you to tell me we're in a precarious position, and I would say that up to this point, I have been a valuable asset to you. I have a good rapport with your grandfather that we may find useful."

Tyler snorted. "Which leads us back to my original area of curiosity. My 'grandfather' wants you for one thing and one thing only."

"And it's a good thing he wants me for something," Amber said. "He puts up with you only because he needs an accountant. As it is, he thinks you're mentally deficient!"

"And whose fault is that?"

"Yours."

"Mine?" He was raising his voice. "How do you figure?"

"I'm sure he found it a bit odd when you couldn't even give him your name." Her voice rose to match his. "Had I not stepped in, he would have had you busted to private and put you on kitchen duty. It's a good thing one of us has the ability to remain in his good graces!"

Tyler glared at her. "The only reason you're in his good graces is because you're prettier than I am. It's certainly not your abilities as a physician that have him groveling at your feet." He clenched his jaw and stood up. "You think that because you're smart you can do anything." He took a step toward the tent flap and turned back, facing her squarely. "Tell me this," he continued. "Have you ever had to fight off a true physical assault by a man twice your size?"

Amber swallowed, unsure of his mood. She realized how very little she actually knew about the man standing before her who was growing more agitated with every word. "Of course not," she answered. "I usually have friends with me when I go out, but—"

"Aha! That's my point. You have friends with you. Who do you have here, Dr. Saxton?" His eyes narrowed and he looked furious. "Who do you have?"

She stared at him, astonished. "No one, obviously! What are you getting at?"

He closed his eyes in frustration. "Let me tell you something. I have a sister who is your size exactly, and there's no way she could hold him off."

Amber shook her head. "Hold who off? What are you talking about?"

Tyler stared at Amber and calmed himself. The angry expression had fled, and into its place slipped a mask of arrogant indifference. "Nothing. I'm going to get some sleep. I'll see you tomorrow." He paused at the entrance. "Enjoy your book." He turned and was gone.

****

Tyler entered his tent, shaking. He was disgusted at his outburst. He couldn't recall ever displaying so much emotion in front of another person. He'd learned early in life that it was to his advantage to hide his thoughts and stay calm, unruffled, and detached. Feelings of hatred and hostility that he buried with his dead father had returned with alarming intensity during dinner with the general. He lay down on his bedroll and closed his eyes, trying to ignore the silver flashes that were the unmistakable prelude to a migraine. He swore aloud when he realized he had no medicine to ease the pain. It would be a long night.

Chapter 11

Amber awoke to the sound of a blaring trumpet. The noise was so loud and piercing that she opened her eyes and bolted upright, convinced that the bugle player must be standing at the foot of her cot. She thought wistfully of her warm shower back home and wondered when she'd get a chance to properly bathe. She felt positively grimy. At least she'd had a chance to wash her hair the evening before she'd left the hospital. Shivering as she rose and attempted to fix the mess her hair had become, she did the best she could with the comb and small "looking glass" Katherine had given her, grumbling as the cold air hit her neck and ears.

"I can't believe women wore their hair up like this in the dead of winter," she muttered aloud as she shoved the pins into place the way Janet and Katherine had taught her. "All in the name of propriety." She smoothed her clothes, which she had slept in, and wrapped her cloak around her shoulders. She lifted her tent flap, still grumbling to herself. "I'd leave my hair down if I didn't think they'd accuse me of being a prostitute."

She ran right into Tyler, who had apparently been standing outside waiting for her. "Do you always talk to yourself so early in the morning?"

"No, I usually wait until evening," she shot back. She stopped when she got a good look at his pale face and the dark circles under his eyes. "You look terrible! What happened?"

"I didn't sleep well." He turned and started toward the general's tent. Amber fairly jogged to keep up with him. She pulled her hood carefully up over her hair, not wanting to have to again tame the wayward strands into submission. Curly hair was one thing when one had a plethora of goopy hair products at one's disposal. Soap and water alone were a bit of a problem.

"Listen, if you're still worried about the general, I'm sure—" Amber began.

"I'm fine," he cut her off. "You're eating with us again, so brace yourself." They stopped at the general's tent and Tyler moved to lift the tent flap. "Remember," he whispered as she entered, "don't provoke him!"

Amber looked at him in annoyance. "How stupid do you think I am?" she whispered.

"You don't want to know," he muttered and shoved her forward to face the general.

****

Breakfast passed much as dinner had the night before. Amber ate in silence and replied only when addressed. The general questioned the men on the status of the camp and soldiers, and in turn briefed them all on recent happenings in other states. Amber wondered why he bothered to include her at all. She held her tongue when she would have liked to ask questions, and grew increasingly depressed and pensive as the meal progressed.

She gave a mental sigh of relief as the men finished eating and the general dismissed them. He turned to Amber and said, "Today you'll meet with Dr. Davis and learn your new duties. I trust you can handle this?"

"Yes, I can handle it," she replied a trifle too sharply. The general's eyes narrowed. She smiled and covered her mistake by extending her hand to him and murmuring, "Forgive me, General. I'm afraid I find myself a bit irritable of late. It must be the weather."

"Of course, my dear." He brought her hand to his lips, his eyes never leaving hers. "I'm sure it won't happen again."

"Of course not."

Major O'Brian entered at the general's command and offered Amber his arm. She took it and discreetly winked at Tyler, who had been eyeing her warily all morning. *Don't worry—I'm handling this!* she wanted to say. Instead, she smiled at Ian and laid the groundwork for a pleasant conversation as they left the tent.

The major took Amber to the camp's "medical station." It consisted of a large tent that housed three makeshift tables, which were actually nothing more than planks of wood resting on boxes and crates. Amber was introduced to Major Davis, a distinguished-looking physician who appeared to be in his early forties. She assumed he had been forewarned of her presence; he was cordial and professional when greeting her. "Heaven knows we can use qualified help," he said as he shook her hand.

Amber appreciated the doctor's reception and nodded her thanks when Ian O'Brian quietly withdrew. She was pleasantly surprised with the attitude of the physician before her, and began to hope that the situation at the camp might prove to be better than that at the hospital. Her newfound optimism was dampened substantially as she listened to Major Davis, who was explaining their current inventory.

"We are often short on formal bandages, so all those that are salvageable, we wash and re-use," he told her.

Amber managed to maintain a bland expression as she made a mental note. *Find more bandages.*

The doctor moved on to a box full of instruments. "These are surgical knives and saws. I assume you know how to amputate?"

Amber nodded and made another mental note. *Find some carbolic.* She decided the time had come to see how receptive the man would be to her ideas. "I wonder, sir, if you would indulge me on a little matter."

He nodded. "Certainly."

She took a deep breath. "While I was at the hospital, I noticed that a new program was in place that called for all the floors and bedding to be meticulously washed to avoid the spread of infection. Colonel Duncan has even taken measures to see that fecal matter from the soldiers too ill to make it to the latrines is properly disposed of. He's doing this to insure that flies and other insects won't spread diseases to the kitchen area." She paused.

"Such notions are fairly new, but yes, I agree," Dr. Davis nodded, prompting her to continue.

"Where I come from, sir, we believe that the medical instruments also require the same meticulous care," she said. "They are thoroughly and completely cleansed following each operation. Our surgeons wear robe-like coverings and masks that are later disposed of, and prior to surgery, our hands are scrubbed completely from fingertip to elbow. We wear sterile surgical gloves that are also disposable."

Amber paused for breath and noted the doubtful expression on the doctor's face. She held up her hand as he began to speak. "Please," she said, "I know that conditions here are different. I realize that at times you have hundreds of wounded men lined up after battle. All I ask is that, if we can manage it, you let me keep large kettles of carbolic acid and boiling water close by to cleanse the instruments after each operation." She hoped she was appealing to his sense of logic, and met his gaze, unwavering. "Amazingly enough, you will lose more men to infection and disease in this war than on the battlefield." She realized she was sounding like a prophetess of doom and began to squirm under the major's scrutinizing gaze.

He finally spoke. "I suppose, time permitting, we can try things your way." He interrupted her expressions of gratitude with some criticism. "Supposing we run short on carbolic. Then what do you suggest?"

"Even a kettle of boiling water would be better than nothing," she offered.

Dr. Davis nodded and sat on a stool, motioning her to sit across from him. "Well, Dr. Saxton, if nothing else you seem to be level-headed. How do you handle crises?"

Amber smiled. "I think you'll find me level-headed, especially in a crisis." Her expression clouded. "I do have one concern . . ." She hesitated, unsure of where the major's loyalties lay.

"What is it?"

"The general has some doubts about my abilities as a physician because of my gender." She stopped.

Dr. Davis smiled. "To be honest, Dr. Saxton, I would probably harbor those same doubts myself, had it not been for your friend."

Amber's ears perked up. "What friend?"

"Captain Kirk paid me a visit this morning. He informed me that you are a very competent physician and are entirely capable, despite your gender disadvantages. The captain seems to be a bright man. The word around camp is that the general highly favors him already. I see no reason not to believe him. I'll be speaking to the general on your behalf to be sure you're allowed to work on the men as a doctor, not a nurse." He smiled.

Amber forced a smile of her own and did her best to appear grateful. "Gender disadvantages," she echoed. "He does have a way with words, doesn't he?"

"I beg your pardon?"

Amber was granted a reprieve from explaining herself as a young man stuck his head inside the tent. "Major Davis, we have a group of men out here that needs to be seen."

The major offered Amber his arm and introduced her to the young soldier. "This is my assistant." The lieutenant saluted, his admiring eyes never leaving Amber as she and the major began examining the soldiers waiting in front of the tent.

****

Tyler looked over the stacks of inventory and supply sheets before him and wished for the hundredth time he had his IBM laptop and Hewlett-Packard business calculator. His thoughts were interrupted as he heard the general's voice outside the tent. "I'll look into it later," he was saying to someone. Tyler gritted his teeth. The similarities between the general and Tyler's own father were astounding.

The general entered the tent and waited expectantly. Tyler dutifully rose and saluted. He sat back down at the general's nod and waited for the man to speak. "I'm impressed, Kirk," he said, and tossed several sheets of paper onto the desk. "You know your work well. As it stands now, I'm also in dire need of a personal assistant. I'm willing to give you the opportunity to prove yourself."

Tyler fought back a smirk. "I'm honored."

The general shot forward and rested his hands on the desk. "I can elevate or destroy your career, boy. I don't like your attitude. If I didn't feel I could use your talents, I'd demote you this very moment. There are men here who would give anything to be in your position. I suggest you watch yourself."

Tyler swallowed his disgust and managed a smooth reply. "Yes, sir. I appreciate the opportunity." He held the general's hostile gaze and carefully schooled his expression.

"Good. I'll expect your full loyalty and compliance," said the general. "I don't like being contradicted."

Tyler again stood and saluted as the general left the tent. He closed his eyes and counted to ten before sitting down and resuming his work.

****

"So, how was your first day at the office, dear?" Amber had endured another dinner with the general and his men in silence. She welcomed the fresh, brisk air outside the tent and inhaled deeply.

Tyler scowled at her question as they began to walk. "I'm now his private executive secretary," he muttered quietly, so as not to be overheard. "I have to do things that were definitely not in the original job description. Had I known, I would never have applied for the position."

Amber stopped walking, her mouth agape. "Why, Captain Kirk! I do believe you have made a subtle attempt at humor! I didn't realize you were capable."

Tyler shot her a dirty look and shoved his hands into the pockets of his overcoat. "Let's go. You're causing a scene."

She smothered a laugh and continued walking. "Do I embarrass you?" she asked, a smile tugging at the corners of her mouth.

He glanced at her, clearly annoyed, and remained silent. She shook her head. "I guess I should shut my mouth or you'll never try to be funny again." Her smile grew as his scowl deepened. "I really should stay on your good side. It's in my best interest to be nice to you."

"Are you always so self-serving?" Tyler asked, one eyebrow quirked.

"Absolutely." She grinned.

Amber stole a sidelong glance at the man walking beside her. He could grace the pages of a number of magazines back in their own time, she mused, yet he didn't have the lanky male-modelish look about him. He was broad through the shoulders, at least six feet tall and carried himself with a certain masculine athleticism that she was sure had broken more than a few female hearts. His face was firmly chiseled with a straight nose, beautiful hazel eyes, and eyelashes a girl would envy. And, a full, sensual mouth . . .

Amber shook herself out of her thoughts with a start. What was wrong with her? She should be concentrating on figuring out how to get back home, or at least how to make things better for the regiment from a medical standpoint, not allowing her mouth to water at the sight of her traveling companion. She spied Major O'Brian talking with a group of men and was grateful for the distraction. "There's Ian. I've been looking for him all day. Excuse me for a minute, will you?"

"Sure," he shrugged and watched her approach O'Brian. Within minutes, she had completely charmed the entire group of men surrounding her. They all looked at her with rapt attention as she smiled and gently teased with them. Soon they were all laughing and looking like prepubescent schoolboys. Tyler found himself growing increasingly annoyed. He didn't know why—she didn't treat him any differently than she treated the others. Maybe that was the problem.

He shook his head, trying to clear his thoughts. Amber eventually turned and addressed Ian specifically. The major nodded and took her arm, then they stepped away from the group. Ian's head was bent toward hers, and they appeared to be deep in conversation. She was a woman well assured of who she was in the world—even a world that wasn't her own. Tyler felt like a fool for observing them, and turned and walked back to the general's tent to finish some paperwork.

Chapter 12

"So, we will begin packing up directly after breakfast. Are there any questions?" The general regarded the men seated with him at the table.

"I have one," Amber spoke clearly. The general turned to her, his eyebrows raised.

"Have provisions been made for the men who are too ill to march?" she asked.

"Miss Saxton, I'm afraid we don't have the resources to pamper every man who feels a bit weak," the general replied, annoyance clearly written across his features.

Amber held her tongue until everyone had left except Tyler and the general. "I wonder, sir," she said when they were alone, "if you are aware that you have men too ill with typhoid to even leave their tents. I recommend they be transferred to a hospital in the area before we leave." She paused. "They'll only slow you down."

The general was staring at her. "You recommend?" he asked incredulously. "*You* recommend?"

Tyler noticed that Amber didn't cower. In fact, she actually moved closer and laid a hand on the general's arm.

"I know, sir, that you are a man of honor. I'm sure you must retire each evening completely exhausted with concern for the welfare of your men. I also understand," she continued in a quiet, placating voice, "that you, among others of course, are responsible for the preservation of the Union and cannot be bothered with . . . trifles." She smiled. "I think only of your emotional welfare and the physical well-being of your men when I suggest that they be moved to a hospital. Surely your mind will be at ease, knowing they are in capable hands."

The general had remained quiet during her speech and impassively studied her face when she finished. He despised manipulative women. He gave her a soft smile and pulled her closer, leaning down to kiss her cheek and lingering just long enough to make her feel uncomfortable. He pulled back, feeling the victor, although no visible emotions played across her face.

"I'll speak with Dr. Davis," he finally said. "You're dismissed." He turned to Tyler. "I have some matters to attend to. See that Miss Saxton receives assistance packing."

Amber watched the general leave and remained silent, not wanting to look at Tyler. He stood behind her, one hand in his pocket, the other massaging his tired eyes. She finally turned to face him. He wanted to throttle her. Instead, he ran his hand across the back of his neck and shook his head. "You're playing with fire. You do realize that?"

She nodded. "I don't know what you expect me to do, though."

Tyler threw up his hands in frustration. "Don't talk to him! Use a mediator. If you have medical concerns, voice them through Davis, or even me." He picked up her cloak and handed it to her. "Come on. We have a lot to do."

****

Amber observed the packing process and was determined to dismantle her own tent. "No, really," she brushed Tyler aside. "I feel like I have to prove something."

She was tense and emotionally exhausted. She had managed to throw herself into her work during the three days that had passed since she and Tyler had joined the camp. She found that her troubles crowded in on her when she tried to get comfortable at night in the small tent. She grew homesick for her old life and asked herself repeatedly why she was there and not where she belonged.

She prayed so frequently that she wondered where one prayer ended and the next began. Her lack of sleep was disconcerting; she was never completely rested and was forced to rely on instinct and years of study to fulfill her medical duties. The challenges were compounded by the fact that she was lacking in modern medical equipment and medicines. Her absent humility was quick in returning.

Amber sighed as she viewed the task before her. "Feel free to jump in, though, if I start floundering too badly." She managed a smile. "When I finish here I'll see if I can help Dr. Davis with anything."

A young boy who didn't look a day older than sixteen years interrupted them. He approached Tyler and saluted. "Sir? Some of the men over here are having a problem."

Amber smiled. The men in the regiment were coming to Tyler for help with problems and concerns. He had natural abilities as a leader and was more approachable than the general, despite the harsh front that Amber noticed Tyler tried so desperately to maintain.

"Where's your squadron leader?" Tyler asked the boy gently.

The young soldier cleared his throat. "I am the squadron leader, sir."

Amber watched Tyler walk with the soldier and wondered how it would have been to meet him under normal circumstances, in their own time. As she folded her tent and observed the other soldiers around her, she realized with dismay that she was the only one with a cot. Everyone else slept in bedrolls on the ground. She hastily snatched up the cot and rushed to the medical tent where Dr. Davis and the medical team's four other physicians were preparing to travel. She hadn't encountered any open hostility or animosity from the four other men, thanks to Dr. Davis' intervention, but she had felt their stares and their reservations as she worked alongside them.

"I'd like to donate this." She extended the cot to Dr. Davis. "I'm sure we'll find a use for it when the time comes."

Davis seemed surprised. "Isn't it yours? I understand the general put you in one of the larger tents usually reserved for high-ranking officers."

Amber flushed. "I don't need it."

Davis accepted the cot from her. "Thank you, Dr. Saxton."

She smiled at the major. "You've known me for several days now and have found me to be a competent colleague, I believe. It may not be altogether proper, but I really wish you would call me Amber."

"Well, in that case, you must call me James."

****

Tyler made his way through throngs of soldiers on his way to the medical station. He needed to be sure Amber was doing well and was ready to move out with the rest of the regiment. *You know she's fine,* his thoughts mocked him as he walked. *You're looking for excuses to see her.* "Well, why shouldn't I?" he muttered aloud, eliciting stares from those he passed.

He clamped his mouth shut. *Why shouldn't I?* He mentally repeated the thought. She was beautiful, brilliant, and funny. Her biting sense of humor almost matched his own, with the possible exception that hers had a soft edge that his was sadly lacking. That she found uses for her sense of humor considering their current circumstance was a quality he found particularly alluring. When was the last time he'd been attracted to a woman because of her sense of humor? Had he ever been?

When he finally found Amber, she was examining an ugly wound on a soldier's arm. Chaos was erupting around them as the camp was preparing to leave, yet Amber acted as though she and the soldier were in the calm privacy of an examining room. He knew she was stressed. He'd seen her not an hour before, pacing in front of her tent and trying to catch her breath. She'd obviously pulled herself together and was stable and solid when she needed to be. He had to admire her for it. If he wasn't careful, he'd have to kiss his "Avoid Emotional Entanglements At All Costs" rule good-bye.

"So, this is a bayonet wound, huh?" She was gently cleaning the area, noticing the obvious signs of infection.

"Yes, ma'am," the soldier answered.

"I understand these are uncommon," Amber continued. "You must have been within close range, Jonathan."

The boy grinned sheepishly and blushed. "Yes. It happened during my first battle. I was so surprised; I never heard the command to retreat. Next thing I knew, a Reb charged right at me with his bayonet. I moved, but not fast enough."

She smiled. "Well, you're still alive to tell the story. That's good."

"Yes, ma'am. It is."

"When did this happen?"

"About three weeks ago."

Amber gently probed the wound, a light frown creasing her brow. "How was it treated when it happened?"

"The doctor cleaned off the dirt and bandaged it up," he told her.

Amber helped the boy remove his arm from the shirt-sleeve, and with a soapy cloth began to gently clean his arm from shoulder to fingers. She talked all the while.

"This may sound strange, but it's very important that you keep this arm clean," she said. "You must wash it every day, just as I am doing now. You also need to keep your clothes as clean as possible. It's been a while since your shirt was washed, hasn't it?"

The boy nodded, and Amber continued. "I'm going to put a clean bandage on the wound. We need to change it every day. Don't do it by yourself, come and find me. Okay?" He nodded again.

Amber patted his arm dry with a clean cloth. "Do you see this yellow stuff? It's puss. You need to keep your arm clean so it doesn't get any worse. Am I making sense?" The boy nodded solemnly.

She bandaged the arm swiftly and carefully, and sent the boy on his way. As she turned to gather the meager supplies she had used, Tyler saw that she looked troubled and concerned. She glanced up as he approached.

"What's wrong?" he asked.

She sighed. "Did you see that boy?"

"I think so—the one you were just with?" Tyler wasn't about to confess that he'd been standing there the entire time, watching her every move.

"Well," she continued, "his arm is a mess. I don't remember when I've seen such a bad infection. He needs a really good antibiotic." She tried to laugh, but the sound was hollow. "What a cruel twist of fate."

"What do you mean?"

She lowered her voice and moved closer. "That I should be dropped here, in the midst of this medical hell, with the knowledge but no resources." She shook her head. "If the war doesn't get that boy, the infection will."

They stood in silence, absorbed in their own thoughts. "Do you really believe in God?" he suddenly asked her.

"Yes," she answered.

"Of course."

"You don't?" she asked, knowing what his answer would be before he offered it.

"No."

She didn't pursue it. She was sure he had his reasons. He offered his arm to her and she took it, trying to hide her surprise. They walked back to their former campsite in silence.

Since meeting the general, Tyler's moods had been unpredictable. He hadn't attempted to touch her in any way since the first night they had met and he'd hauled her away from the infection-spreading Dr. Matthews. She could understand his depression, however, as no one else could. Though her panic attacks were lessening, she felt constantly on edge herself.

****

Amber gratefully accepted the biscuits Tyler handed her. They had been marching for five hours and she was famished. The word among the men was that their destination was Tennessee. Amber could only be grateful for the fact that they were heading south, and hopefully for warmer weather. She did her best not to think about the fact that each step took them closer to the enemy. She rested against a gnarled tree trunk, thankful for a short break, and leaned back, closing her eyes and recalling the events of the morning.

The general had supplied Tyler with an enormous war horse and suggested that Amber ride with him. She was about to accept when she happened to notice a soldier with a severe limp who was marching with as much dignity as he could muster.

"I can't," she whispered to Tyler. "My conscience would eat me alive." He followed her gaze and connected with her train of thought, experiencing his own pangs of guilt.

"You ride the horse, I'll walk," he told her.

"No!" she hissed. "I'm in perfectly good health. I did the stair machine for an hour every day at home."

He raised his eyebrows. "Outside, in the cold, wearing combat boots and a long woolen dress?"

In the end, they offered the horse to the limping soldier and insisted he accept it graciously. All was well, until the general realized that neither Tyler nor Amber was riding the magnificent animal he had so generously provided. Amber realized that Tyler's impressions of the general were entirely accurate as he roared at Tyler and humiliated the soldier.

Amber pulled herself to the present and opened her eyes. She looked at Tyler, perplexed.

"What?" he asked.

"I don't understand why the general has always been so open around me. He invites me to eat with him and he discusses military objectives while I'm sitting there," she said between bites. "I could be a spy, for all he knows!"

Tyler snorted. "I think lust has clouded his judgment."

Amber raised her eyebrows. "Then how do we explain his immediate acceptance of you?"

Tyler shrugged. "I'm a likable guy."

"That's a lie!" Amber laughed as he scowled at her, having taken mock offense. Her smile faltered as the general approached. The more she grew to dislike him, the harder it became to maintain pleasant pretenses.

The general addressed Amber first. "My dear, I apologize if my gruff behavior this morning was offensive to you. I forget, at times, that we have a lady within the regiment. My temper can be quite frightening to those of the weaker sex."

Amber swallowed a sarcastic commentary on his overblown sense of self and smiled. "Not at all, sir. I am not timid by nature."

"How fortunate for you."

Tyler shot Amber a warning glance and she acquiesced, ending the verbal combat. The general turned to Tyler. "I want you on that horse and in front of the line with me in five minutes. I need to discuss some things with you." In an undertone, he added, "I really do prefer that she ride with you, which is why I provided you with the largest horse in the regiment. That horse has carried men who weigh more than the two of you combined. I don't need her fainting from fatigue or distracting the men." He turned on his heel and left.

Amber pasted a brittle smile on her face as the general retreated. "Does he think I'm hard of hearing?"

"I don't think he cared if you heard him or not." Tyler strolled to the tree where the horse was tied and called over his shoulder, "So are you walking or riding?"

"I think I'll walk." She was tempted to ride but wasn't sure she wanted to be in such close proximity to Tyler. Best to keep her wits about her, she assured herself. Maybe in another place, another time . . . She had to smirk at the irony.

He grinned at her as though reading her thoughts, and she caught her breath. She had rarely seen him smile. "Suit yourself," he said and mounted the horse. "Just be careful."

She shook her head as she watched him ride off and smiled ruefully to herself. He was making her heart pound.

"Dr. Saxton!" Amber turned as her name was called, and she gratefully fell in step next to several men who assisted the medical team. As the line slowly moved forward, Amber grumbled and picked up her skirt to keep from tripping over it. It was definitely too long to walk in comfortably.

They had been marching for an hour when Amber saw the general approaching at a full gallop, with Tyler close behind. Amber had been amusing the men with embarrassing, yet time-generic tales from her childhood, which they had all seemed to find extremely funny. The laughter and good-natured bantering died away as the general drew near, his face red with fury.

"Is this the way you've been trained?" he roared at the men. "To sit here and laugh like women? What will you do if we're ambushed? Share your jokes with the enemy?"

The men sobered instantly and Amber felt increasingly awkward for being the cause of their distress. The general guided his horse toward her. "I knew you would be a problem," he glowered at her. "You're riding with me."

Before Amber could even blink, Tyler had maneuvered his horse to stand between her and the general. He extended his hand down to her and hauled her up in front of him, all the while speaking in a low voice to the man shaking in fury before him. "Sir, allow me. You really must remain mobile, should the need arise, and she would only be a hindrance," he explained.

Amber adjusted herself in the uncomfortable position and tried to look contrite. "I apologize, sir. I didn't realize I was placing the men in jeopardy." The general glared at her.

Tyler tightened his arm around her waist in warning and met the general's gaze above her head. "It won't happen again, sir."

The general took a deep breath in a visible attempt to calm himself. "I'm sure it won't," he said and turned his mount.

Amber turned to look at the soldiers who were trying not to stare. "I'm so sorry," she began, looking miserable. "I —"

Tyler tugged on the reins and headed back to the front of the line before she could finish. "I was trying to apologize to them!"

"Be quiet, Amber," Tyler muttered through clenched teeth.

She shook her head in frustration. "I don't believe this. None of us were doing anything wrong. I was trying to make this whole ordeal a little less tedious for them."

"Well that's just wonderful," Tyler growled in her ear, "but the idea here is for us to stay *out* of the limelight!"

Amber said nothing further, but tried in vain to get comfortable on the horse. The saddle was enormous and logistically could have served them both efficiently, but Tyler had yanked her upon the animal with such haste that she hadn't had time to situate herself accordingly. As it was, the horn stabbed roughly into her right leg and her left leg hung down uncomfortably. She wasn't about to mention that fact to her riding companion, whose anger was physically palpable.

Tyler guided the horse to the front of the line and reined in beside the general, who acknowledged their presence with an irritated glance. They had ridden for some time in relative silence when the general ordered those on horseback to disburse and ride back through the regiment to "assure the safety of the men."

All but one man turned aside to follow the order, and Tyler watched with interest as Major Edwards, a sly, groveling man in his late thirties, urged his horse forward at the almost imperceptible nod of the general.

"What are you looking at?" Amber asked.

"I'm not sure. Possibly nothing," Tyler replied absently.

"Well, I now know that romance novels are complete and utter farces," Amber grumbled, still trying to shift into a more comfortable position.

Tyler finally turned his attention to her. "What?"

She shook her head and smiled ruefully. "In all the romance novels I've read, the hero and heroine ride off together on the same horse, blissfully happy."

"So?"

"There's no way they could have been happy sharing a horse," Amber replied, tucking a stray hair behind her ear. "I've never been so uncomfortable in my entire life."

"Are these the novels I see in the grocery store with half-naked people on the covers?" Tyler was amused.

She nodded, blushing slightly. He was amazed. He'd never seen her embarrassed before.

"You mean the ones where the man's hair is as long as the woman's and the man always looks like Fabio?" he goaded.

She laughed. "The man usually *is* Fabio." She twisted to look at him. "What?" she asked, exasperated.

He looked incredulous. "I'm surprised you read books like that. I would have thought you had more taste. What a disappointment."

"What do you mean, 'books like that'? I'll have you know that the majority of women who do read romance novels are college graduates and extremely bright! A lot of quality research goes into those books, they're as well-written as any book in any other genre, and heaven forbid we should read something with a guaranteed happy ending . . ." She would have continued her tirade, except she looked at his grinning face and realized he was teasing her.

She shook her head, feeling sheepish, and laughed. "Actually, if you want to know the truth," she said, "I started reading romance novels my first year of medical school. I used to get so tired of medical textbooks, and I had convinced myself that for entertainment, I should be reading depressing literary classics. Those are all well and good, but sometimes it's too much."

She smiled. "I was lying on my bed one afternoon with a splitting headache, and my roommate said to me, 'Amber, you need an entertaining diversion.' I said, 'Camille, I don't have time for a man.' She just laughed and tossed me a copy of a novel she'd been reading and said, 'This is better than a man. You can read it in a few hours and then get on with your life a much happier person.'"

Tyler laughed. "So, most people have meaningful relationships, but you have romance novels."

Amber smiled again. "Something like that. What about you? What do you have in the place of a meaningful relationship?"

He raised his eyebrows in surprise. "What makes you think I don't have a meaningful relationship?"

"I don't know. I can't picture you in that setting, I guess," said Amber. "You're more like the Marlboro Man. You know, just the lone man and his horse; the kind of guy who stops into town, has a brief encounter with one of the town's more popular women, and then rides off on his horse alone—which, I might add, would actually be much more comfortable than having to take her with him."

Tyler shrugged, trying to appear nonchalant. "So, what's wrong with that?" He was disturbed that she had been able to read him so easily.

"Nothing, if you don't mind being alone."

"It seems to work for you."

"What makes you think I don't have someone?"

He snorted. "If you had a boyfriend, you'd probably be blubbering all over the place because you miss him so much, and you wouldn't flirt with every single man in the regiment."

She looked back at him in surprise. "You think I flirt?"

He smirked. "That's actually a mild way of putting it."

"What, exactly, are you saying?" she asked.

"That you're very . . . friendly," he replied. "And I think you're used to getting attention from men. What kind of attention, I couldn't say . . ."

Amber cut him off. "I can't believe you. It just so happens that I like people, and there are no women here for me to interact with. That does not mean I take off into the bushes with every man in the regiment!"

"If you say so. I have no way of knowing what you do when I'm not around."

She was fuming. "You ask any man here, and he'll tell you I'm the very epitome of propriety. I'm gracious and open and friendly and honest. You're just moody and antisocial. You're friendly one minute and insulting the next." She looked over her shoulder to be sure no one overheard. "And don't feed me some excuse about being all weirded out with this time flip-flop thing. I get the feeling that this is how you were at home."

He knew he'd offended her, but had no idea what he should say. He had no recollection of ever sincerely apologizing to anyone. They rode until dusk in virtual silence.

Chapter 13

When the regiment stopped for the night, Amber dismounted and went in search of the medical staff. When she finally found them, they were already surrounded by a group of soldiers that was growing larger by the minute. The complaints varied from diarrhea to festering wounds, and a horrible, raspy sounding cough was spreading around the camp with alarming speed. The doctors assisted where they could and offered meager advice when there were no available cures.

It was dark when the line finally died down and Amber was able to consider dinner. She was putting some supplies in a box when she heard footsteps behind her. "James?" she said over her shoulder. "Have you seen the carbolic?"

"It's me, Amber." Tyler stepped forward out of the shadows.

"Oh. I thought you were Dr. Davis." She finished filling the box and stood, brushing invisible wrinkles from her dress.

"Amber, I . . . ," he paused, fumbling for words. She did nothing to ease his discomfort. "I owe you an apology," he finally said. "I made some comments earlier about your character that were inappropriate and unfair. I'm not very good at saying I'm sorry, but I am sorry and I just wanted you to know that."

He was tense and uncomfortable, yet he didn't know why it was so important to him that she accept his apology. Immediately after setting up camp, he'd had a meeting with the general, followed by scores of complaints and requests for assistance from the soldiers. Through it all, the knowledge that he'd offended Amber had nagged at him until he could hardly concentrate.

Now, he stood before her feeling extremely vulnerable and foolish. She took pity on him. "I made a slur against your character a few days ago, when we were riding to meet up with the regiment. I guess I deserved a slam in return," she finally said.

"No, you didn't. I was rude. It was uncalled for." He moved forward. "Have you eaten yet?"

She shook her head and rubbed her eyes. "I haven't had time."

He turned her by the shoulders and gently propelled her forward, his hand on her back. "Come on," he said. "I set your tent up over here by mine. I couldn't find your cot, though."

"I donated it to medicine," she replied wryly.

He stopped walking and looked at her, surprised. "Why?"

She lifted her hands and shrugged in exasperation. "Nobody else has one; I don't need one either. Why is everyone so shocked?"

Tyler resumed walking, but continued to regard her intently. "I am not fragile!" she said. "I can sleep on the ground like everyone else. You don't have a cot either."

"Of course I don't, but yours was a gift from the general himself." He stopped before her tent, still looking confused. "Is this a gender equality thing?"

"No!" She couldn't help laughing in amazement. "I am perfectly healthy and robust. There are wounded and sick men here who will benefit more from its use than I will. I wasn't getting any sleep on it anyway."

He finally shrugged. "It's your decision." He motioned to a log placed outside of a circle of stones and told her to sit. He then proceeded to build a fire within the stones, conscious of her watchful gaze.

"Looks like the Boy Scout program served you well," she said when he had coaxed a flame from tinder only half dry.

"Believe it or not, I learned this in basic training." He reached for a tin pot full of beans and suspended it over the fire.

Amber was shocked. "You mean you really are in the Army?"

He shot her a dirty look. "Navy, not Army. I'm not active anymore. I was in for five years as a pilot."

She raised her eyebrows. "Will wonders never cease? You're a pilot?"

He nodded. "I got my license when I was a teenager. I graduated from Embry Riddle Aeronautical University in Florida and then went on to Officer Training School. I decided I needed a change and got out three years ago."

"So what are you doing now?"

"I went back to graduate school for an M.B.A., and now I work for an accounting firm in D.C."

How was it that she had never asked him what he did for a living? She realized she had been too busy walking around in a daze to wonder about the details of his life. "Why on earth did you devote so much time to a career as a pilot and then change your mind?"

Tyler was silent for a moment. When he finally spoke, it was with a certain amount of reluctance. "I chose a career in flying and the military originally to annoy my father. He saw me graduating me from an Ivy League school and becoming a high-powered attorney. I couldn't stand the thought of doing anything he would approve of. I went the military route, and after he died, I decided to do something else."

"So what did he say when you told him you were joining the Navy?"

"He nearly had a stroke." Tyler looked grim. "I wouldn't have been disappointed." He paused and studied her face. "I don't expect you to understand."

Amber looked thoughtful. "You're a bright man," she said softly. "What I don't understand is why you would waste so much time doing something you didn't truly want to do, just to spite someone else."

"It wasn't a total waste. I learned a lot, and I do love flying." He shrugged in dismissal. "We all do things we regret. Chalk it up to experience."

He took the beans off the fire and dished them into a small tin plate. He handed them to her with a cup of steaming liquid. She smiled. "I'll be sure to work late every night if it means you'll faithfully serve me dinner."

"Ha," he scoffed. "Don't get used to this." He watched her attempt to eat the mediocre food without gagging. "So, Dr. Saxton. Don't you think it's time you told me your story?"

"What story?"

"What story?" he mimicked. "How does a prepubescent become a physician? That story."

Amber laughed. "Okay, let's have it. How old do you think I am?"

"Nineteen, maybe twenty," he guessed.

"I'm twenty-five."

"Oh, my mistake," Tyler laughed. "You're practically a spinster."

She shook her head. "Actually, there are some who would consider me a spinster."

"So, you were a child prodigy?"

She looked uncomfortable. "I don't like that terminology." She stared absently at her dinner, not wanting to answer him.

"Did I say something wrong?" he asked. He added a small log to the fire and glanced at her curiously.

She gave a short laugh and shook her head. "People treat me differently after I tell them about my academic history."

"I promise I'll be just as rude to you as I've always been."

She took a deep breath and let it out on a sigh, appreciative of his attempt at humor. "My father is a history professor and my mother is an R.N. I have one sister, Elizabeth, who's going to school at the University of Washington. My parents put a lot of time into our educations. They read to us before we could talk and saved their money so they could take us on trips all over the world.

"I've always liked to learn and was in accelerated programs growing up, so I graduated from high school when I was fifteen. I was able to test out of a lot of stuff, and I did my undergrad in two years. Medical school I did in the usual four years, then there was my two-year internship, and I'm now a second-year resident." She put a spoonful of beans in her mouth, chewed briefly and swallowed. "That's my story."

Tyler closed his mouth. It had fallen open halfway through her speech. He tried to think of something casual to say but was at a loss for words. Amber's eyebrows drew together in a frown. "I knew it."

Tyler grinned. "I had no idea I was in the presence of intellectual greatness. You hide it very well."

Amber laughed. "Well, thank you. I try."

"So you read romance novels because you don't have time for men, basically," he said.

"There haven't been many," she admitted. "Not necessarily because there wasn't time, though."

"Meaning?"

"The timing itself was always off. The guys on my academic level were years older than I was, and the guys my own age thought I was weird. I had one boyfriend that I was quite in love with about three years ago, but he got tired of me." She smiled. "Chalk it up to experience," she said, borrowing his phrase.

He smiled softly in response, examining a cut on his finger.

"I am curious about something," she said.

"What's that?"

"I know it's none of my business, but you seem to have some hang-ups about your father," she observed, wondering if she was broaching a topic best left alone. "Have you ever talked to anyone about it?"

"Why, are you a shrink on the side?"

"Maybe I am."

"My father is dead now, so it doesn't matter."

Amber was silent for a moment. "Your father may be dead, but you aren't. I was just thinking you might enjoy life a little more if you didn't have so much to carry around."

"I enjoy life," Tyler said flatly.

"No, you don't." Her tone was soft, without a trace of flippancy or malice.

He wasn't surprised by her gentle honesty; in fact, he'd come to expect it. "I've learned how to deal with things in my own way. I don't want someone else mucking around in my head, digging up things I'd rather leave alone."

She changed the subject. "You never did tell me how old you are."

"You never asked."

"I'm asking. How old are you? Forty-five?" She smirked at the look of annoyance he shot her way.

"I'm thirty, thank you very much."

"A wise old man, huh?"

"Older and wiser than you are," he smiled.

"You mentioned a sister once," Amber continued. "Is she older or younger?"

"You don't forget much, do you?" he said.

"Never." Amber smiled.

"She's younger," Tyler finally answered.

"What's she like?" asked Amber.

Tyler was thoughtful for a moment. "She's independent, tough," he paused, smiling, "and rich. She shunned the family money and made herself into a very successful interior designer." He shrugged. "Other than my mother, she's the only woman I've ever trusted. Every other woman I've known has either lied or schemed her way into or out of my life." He stopped talking, inwardly appalled. Why on earth had he told her that?

Amber saved him from embarrassment by leaving his comments alone. They fell into a comfortable silence, and she gazed out at the small fires dotting the camp. She was extremely tired and cold. Shivering, she picked up the mug Tyler had given her, which was still steaming.

"You'll warm up a little if you drink that, you know. It's really not that bad," Tyler suggested.

"Maybe later."

"Or maybe not at all? I do know that Mormons don't drink coffee, which I think is absurd. I'm waiting to see how long your dedication holds out."

She smiled good-naturedly. "As long as I can stand it."

"Everyone here drinks coffee," he said. "I've watched you at every meal, and you always decline. What have you been doing for liquid?"

"I've been boiling water and drinking two quarts of it daily. And spending a lot of time in the latrine, such as it is." She grimaced.

"What is the big deal about coffee? The caffeine?"

"Well . . . I can't claim to avoid it strictly because of the caffeine. I drank a six-pack of Diet Coke a day back home," she admitted ruefully. "I've had some serious headaches these past few days." She smiled to herself. "Camille would totally rub it in my face if she could."

"So what is it, then?" he pressed.

She sighed, knowing she was discussing a subject most people didn't understand. "We've been told that it's not particularly good for the body and advised to stay away from it. We avoid things that are addicting." She grinned. "Like Diet Coke, I guess."

"So other than a penchant for carbonation, you're obedient to a fault?"

"Part of living a religion involves faith. And no, I'm not always so obedient. I've ignored church counsel before and lived to regret it." Her face reddened for an instant.

"Have you talked to anyone about it?" He now borrowed her phrase, and smiled when she laughed softly.

"Yes, as a matter of fact, and it wasn't pleasant." She noticed his eager smirk and sighed, knowing he wanted to hear all the sordid details. "It involved some . . . stuff that happened with the boyfriend I mentioned."

His expression sobered. "What did he do to you?"

"Nothing," she hastily explained. "He didn't do anything *to* me, exactly. In fact, I was altogether too willing to comply." She leaned closer to the fire and braced her elbows on her knees, her hands still clutching the mug of coffee. "He at least left my virginity intact, if not my pride or my virtue as a whole." Her voice was low and quiet. "I can't blame him, though. One thing my parents never told me was how enjoyable it is. I was caught completely by surprise. The whole situation left me feeling a little defensive. I guess that's why I got so upset at what you implied earlier."

He watched the firelight play on her beautiful face and found himself wishing he could help her shake off the somber mood they'd created so she'd smile at him again.

She looked at him, embarrassed that she had divulged so much. "Well. This seems to be the night for telling secrets."

He shrugged, hoping to ease her discomfort. "There are worse things that could happen." *Much worse*, he mused, mentally shaking his head. He would never understand organized religion.

She nodded, then shivered involuntarily and yawned. "I suppose."

"You know," she continued slowly and reluctantly, broaching a subject she'd been mulling over since joining the regiment, "we spend a lot of time apart during the day. Either one of us could disappear and go back home, leaving the other stranded here . . ."

"I've been thinking about that myself," he admitted quietly. "Here's the thing, though—we arrived here the same day, possibly the same time, and as much as it pains me to admit this, there seems to be some cosmic reason behind what's happened." He took a deep breath. "I don't think we have to worry that one of us will get left behind—I'm pretty sure we'll go together. My only concern now is whether or not I'll live when we get home."

She closed her eyes, knowing he was referring to the fact that when she'd first seen him, he'd been in the ER suffering from a gunshot wound. She cleared her throat. "You weren't beyond hope, you know. In fact, I personally know the trauma surgeons on call that night . . ." She stopped, wanting to offer comfort without sounding trite. "When we get home, I'll see to it that you get the best possible care."

He nodded. "I wonder, though, if there's not some way I can just avoid getting shot in the first place."

Amber offered a half-smile. "Well, now, that would be ideal, wouldn't it?" She laughed hollowly. "At least we know you make it home. You apparently returned before I ever even left. We may have arrived *here* at the same time, but we didn't leave home at the same time. We have no way of knowing if I'll make it back at all."

He shook his head curtly. "Don't start thinking like that. My guess is the whole thing happens instantaneously. Whoever discovers me probably will do so in my office, right where I was when I 'left'."

Amber nodded. "Your friend Derek found you on the floor in your office, shot in the stomach."

"Great." His expression was understandably grim. "Where were you? What's the last thing you remember?"

Her brow creased in thought. "I walked into a door," she said slowly, nodding. "How's that for impressive? I walked into a door, and that's the last thing I remember."

Tyler smiled. "Well, I hope you come to quickly. You'll probably wake up right after you passed out. All I ask is that you hurry up and recover so you can help save my sorry life."

Amber stared into the flickering light. "How do I know this isn't a strangely intense dream?" she whispered, her eyes cloudy and unfocused.

Tyler moved closer to her and pried one hand from her mug. His shoulder touched hers and his thigh brushed up against her leg. She tore her gaze from the fire and looked questioningly into his face. His expression was as solemn as it was bewildered.

"I can't make sense of this," he whispered as he interlaced their fingers, "but I do know it's for real. I think if we forget that, we'll be placing ourselves in danger. There's something we're supposed to do here, and once we figure out what it is, maybe we can be done with all this and go home." He held their clasped hands up in front of her face. "Still think it's a dream? Can't you feel this?"

Her heart thumped in her chest. She nodded slowly. "Yes. I can feel it." She tried for a smile that she couldn't quite manage. "I'm glad you're here with me." The admission manifested itself as a whisper more husky than she'd ever have intentionally uttered.

He mentally cursed their closeness as his body reacted to her presence. He looked for a long time at her fingers, which were so naturally interlaced with his own. It would be so easy to blur the lines between fantasy and reality. He'd been sharing her company and observing her work for only a week, yet he felt closer to her than he had to any woman in recent history. To say he found her physically attractive as well as emotionally so would have been a laughable understatement. She was utterly beautiful.

With eyes closed and a self-mocking smile on his lips, he made a mental effort to cool his raging blood. He patted the back of her hand with his free one, released her and then stood, ending the quiet intimacy. "Come on," he said. "We both need some sleep. Maybe we'll wake up at home."

Amber had to smile. He'd been saying that every night now since they'd met. "Yeah, right."

He took her mug and threw the contents on the fire. Lifting her tent flap, he waited while she entered and situated her bedroll, watching her thoughtfully.

"Nobody would have thought less of you for sleeping on a cot, you know," he said.

"I would have," she replied.

Chapter 14

Amber sat hemming her dress by her small campfire. The regiment had been marching for a week now, and Amber's patience with the long skirt had come to an unequivocal end when she tripped on it and fell, taking the soldier next to her down in the process.

She had been able to convince the general to let her walk at least in the mornings and promised she wouldn't be the cause of any disruptions. She tried to stay active and moved around within the regiment as much as she could, walking with different groups of men every day and discussing their medical problems, home life, or whatever they seemed content to tell her. They respected her because they knew she was close to Tyler, and they respected Tyler unconditionally.

As Amber sat sewing her dress, she reflected on the activities of the week that had passed. The regiment had traveled through many small southern towns along the way, each alike in that they had been tapped of all but the basest of resources with which to sustain their weary inhabitants. The regiment was consistently met with dislike and distrust, although because of their sheer numbers they never experienced any undue confrontations.

One village stood out in Amber's memory with such vivid detail that she knew she'd never be free of its trappings. It seemed a town like many the regiment had passed before, unremarkable in any specific way, except that it seemed to hold Ian O'Brian's attention more acutely than had the rest.

When Amber had questioned him as to his thoughts, he'd replied, "My father's sister, her daughter and grandchildren live in this town. I was hoping for an opportunity to see them." He had been granted his wish as the regiment had set up camp a mere quarter mile from the borders of the small town. The stay was brief—merely two days and nights before beginning the journey again, but Ian had taken the first opportunity afforded him to search out his relatives.

Amber had accompanied him at the reluctant approval of the general. Tyler had been busy with other matters at the time; Amber knew he'd be angry she'd left the regiment, but she couldn't stifle her curiosity about the actual lives of the people so close at hand. *Besides,* she'd thought irritably, *I don't have to answer to him. I'm a twenty-five-year-old physician, not a child.*

Amber and Ian had cautiously approached the outskirts of the town and didn't have to search long before finding the correct address. Ian had paused at the door, apparently searching for an effective way to express his thoughts. "These people don't like me," he finally blurted out, his brow drawn in weary resignation. "Our reception here may not be the warmest."

Before Amber could summon a reply, Ian had knocked on the door of his aunt's home with resolute determination. The door opened a crack; Amber's and Ian's gazes both dropped from the average adult height they'd expected down to the reality of their "host," who'd proven to be a child of approximately six years. The door opened wider to reveal that the child was dressed in clean, if somewhat worn clothes; he had light brown skin and large brown eyes.

"May I help you?" the child ventured.

Amber blinked against the sting of moisture in her eyes. Her friend Camille had a nephew who so resembled the child standing before her that she was hard-pressed not to believe she was at a family reunion with Camille in her own time. She knelt at the child's level. "We're looking for a lady named Helen Porter. Does she live here?"

The child nodded. "She's my grandmother."

"Jeremy, who's at the door?" A clipped voice from inside had the boy turning his head.

Amber straightened as the door was opened wider to reveal a small woman dressed in a plain tan dress adorned by small, faded flowers that had probably once been an attractive pink. The woman eyed the pair dressed in Union Army finery on her doorstep with obvious disgust. "Didn't you people take enough the last time you went through?"

Ian cleared his throat. "Aunt Helen, it's me—Ian."

The woman's eyes widened in shock, then eventually narrowed, the expression on her face doing little to mask her apparent feelings of contempt. "Well, well, well. It's the family Mormon." Helen paused at the insistent tugging on her hand. Her expression softened as she looked into the face of her grandson. "Go find your sister, Jeremy. I'll be there shortly."

Ian's aunt waited until the small boy had disappeared into the house before she again turned to her visitors. "What is it you want?" she asked Ian bluntly. "Have you come by to introduce one of your wives?"

Ian flushed. "Aunt Helen, I merely came by to see if you need help in any way. I'll be in the area for two days," he gestured lamely. "I just thought that if you needed anything . . . well, I heard of your husband's death . . ."

Helen interrupted with a harsh laugh. "And you supposed, since there are no men here, that we're barely living?" She straightened herself to her full height of five feet, one inch. "We're just fine. We don't need Mormon help." She moved to close the door, and as an apparent afterthought, added in a softer tone, "Say hello to my brother for me when you see him next." She quietly but firmly closed the door.

Ian stood for a moment looking at the humble, yet well-maintained home before quietly beginning the walk beside Amber back to the camp. Amber noted the condition of the small town as they left; homes shabby in appearance dotted the streets. Helen Porter's home was a veritable castle in comparison to some. A small group of children, bedraggled and dirty, played in the roadway while weary mothers watched Ian and Amber warily from porches that sagged in disrepair. Amber saw one man as they walked and estimated his age to be at least seventy. The notable absence of male presence was remarkable.

Amber walked in silence, respecting Ian's need for private thought. They had nearly reached the outskirts of the town when he finally spoke.

"I'm sorry to have subjected you to that, Amber." Ian shook his head. "My father's family didn't approve of my baptism or my mother's. My father didn't object too strongly, but he didn't share our views, either. I just wish . . . ," he sighed. "My Aunt Helen's family has had a hard time. Her husband wasn't a kind man; I suspect his death has been something of a relief to my aunt. Her daughter lived with some family friends in New York for a while several years ago, and while there she married an abolitionist—a freed slave."

He paused. "The family was scandalized, of course. Aunt Helen was less upset than the rest, though, I think. When her son-in-law was killed last year, she welcomed her daughter and grandchildren home with open arms. I'm happy for the children's sake, although I can't help but wonder how she keeps them from those who would do them harm. Perhaps she claims to own them—I don't know. I can't help thinking they'd be safer in New York."

He paused again, smiling wryly. "I've felt a certain kinship with my cousin; she married a black man and I joined the Mormons. We both know what it's like to be ostracized."

Amber smiled softly. "It must have taken tremendous courage for your cousin to follow her heart. I was wondering about little Jeremy's appearance. Your explanation makes sense."

Ian nodded and stole a sidelong glance at Amber. "I know you probably don't understand," he paused. "I don't expect anyone to understand—nobody ever does with any degree of compassion . . ."

"I understand perfectly, Ian." She chose her next words carefully. "In my homeland, we've had a history of racial tension and turmoil that has spanned generations. My dear friend Camille," she paused as tears gathered. "She's an African-American. She's black. She joined the Church two years ago. I didn't think she ever would. Her parents are now investigating the Church as well, and I think someday her brother might." A single tear slipped down Amber's cheek as she slowly blinked. "It makes me sick to think of Camille living here, now, in the South . . ." Her breath caught and another tear traced a course down her cheek. She knew perfectly well that conditions in certain areas of the country in her own time were still horrifically tainted by bigotry, but at least at the dawn of the twenty-first century, Camille stood a chance. In the South of 1862, she'd have been in shackles.

Ian nodded soberly. "Your friend is lucky," he said.

"Yes." Amber wearily wiped at her face as her tears fell in earnest, her heart aching at the fate that could have been Camille's. "Yes, she's been blessed."

They had returned to the camp before Tyler knew she'd been gone. She retired directly to her tent and sat for a long time as tears poured down her face, thinking of Camille and her family.

At home, one of her favorite pieces of art was a painting she'd bought for herself and Camille to enjoy; it was a gentle image of the Savior sitting with four children of varied race and culture. It showed the children standing closely around Jesus. Two children stood at his right side—a young girl of Hispanic descent at his elbow with her hands resting on his arm, and a small Caucasian boy standing closely at his side with his hands on the Savior's shoulder. Jesus' left arm encircled a young girl of Asian descent, and his gaze rested lovingly on the small African-American boy standing at his knee, his free hand resting atop that of the boy.

The poignancy and sweetness of the picture had not been lost on Amber when she'd first spied it in an LDS bookstore on one of her visits back home with her parents, nor had it escaped Camille when Amber had presented it with a misty smile. Camille had cried as well; the friends had shared tender tears together and found a place of honor for it in their home amongst other more expensive pieces of art. It would always be Amber's favorite depiction of the Savior.

****

Amber jerked back to the present as the general approached and laid his hand on her shoulder. "My dear, you are the very picture of domestic tranquillity and loveliness."

Had such a statement come from anyone else, she might have been amused. As it was, she gritted her teeth and remained silent, not wanting to say anything to incur his wrath. She was comfortable with her routine and didn't want to jeopardize her walking privileges or be forced to ride daily with him instead of Tyler. The general was unaware of her growing rapport with the men, for she made sure he never saw her laughing or talking with anyone while they were marching.

The general mistook her silence for humility, and leaned forward in an attempt to kiss her cheek. "General!" Tyler barked from Montgomery's tent less than twenty yards away. "Shouldn't we get started? I've gathered your men together, and they're waiting inside."

"Of course," the general answered, annoyed. He turned to Amber and offered her his arm. "I wonder if you would like to join us, my dear. Captain Kirk is about to be promoted."

Amber stuffed the dress she was hemming into her bag and stood to take the general's arm. "I would be delighted, sir."

As they progressed toward the tent, Amber willed herself not to gag. The more she observed the general, the harder-pressed she was to find any positive qualities. She knew he was married, yet his innuendoes toward her were unmistakable. He inspired nothing but fear in his men; Amber had learned this much in conversation with the troops. They harbored no feelings of respect or affection for him; instead they bonded together and went to men like Tyler for help.

Amber was offered a chair as she entered the tent. She watched with some amusement as "Captain James T. Kirk" was promoted to the rank of major. The general finished pinning the emblem on Tyler's uniform coat and slapped him on both shoulders. "Good work, boy!" he bellowed.

Amber was invited to stay for the rest of the meeting. She realized with sudden clarity that the general didn't see her as a threat to security because he didn't think her bright enough to understand the discussions. The man really was an idiot, she decided.

She listened as the plans to approach Grand Junction, Tennessee, were presented. "I received word today that the city has been secured. We'll join General Grant there and proceed with our plans for Vicksburg," the general was saying.

Vicksburg! Of course! Amber had been trying in vain to remember what little she could about 1862 and the direction they were headed. She remembered her father once saying something about General Grant's attacks on Vicksburg, Mississippi, which were never actually successful until July of 1863.

The shock must have registered on her face; Tyler was looking at her with a questioning expression. She mouthed the word, "Later," and paid close attention to the rest of the meeting.

When they were dismissed, Amber made small talk with Ian, who seemed more interested in her each day. She found his attention flattering. He was charming, thoughtful, and very attractive.

She was asking him about his home life when Tyler took her arm and said to Ian, "Will you excuse us please? I need to speak to Amber privately." Without waiting for a response, he ushered her outside and began walking toward their tents, which were side by side, as had become customary.

"Tyler, stop it!" she hissed. "You're acting like a Neanderthal!"

He didn't stop walking until they reached the tent. He opened the flap and urged her inside. She was furious. He looked amused. "Are you angry with me, Amber?"

Her eyes blazed. "I am not your property, Tyler Montgomery. You have no claim on me!" As she whirled around and turned to leave, he caught her arm, his expression sobering.

"Amber, wait. Let me say something." She stopped expectantly and he took a deep breath. "O'Brian is much too interested in you."

"What are you, my father?" she growled.

"Amber, be reasonable," Tyler said. "Imagine the implications of getting involved with someone here. What happens when you go back?"

"Who said anything about getting involved? He is very sweet and attentive. I enjoy his company. Besides, I'm beginning to wonder if we're *ever* going back."

He ignored the last. "You're toying with him. The man is obviously attracted to you, and you're using him as a diversion to amuse yourself."

"I am not!"

"Keep your voice down."

Amber turned her back to him and put her hand on her forehead, trying to calm herself. She didn't want to admit that he could be right.

"Are you in love with him, Amber?" His voice was soft.

She sighed. "No."

"Then leave him alone."

She whirled around. "I can't talk to him because I'm not in love with him? I'm not going to become a social recluse just to keep you happy. These men enjoy my company."

Tyler shook his head and smirked. "I've always assumed a big ego was prerequisite to being a physician. I see you fit the mold just fine."

"I could say the same for fighter pilots," she shot back.

They stood glaring at each other, neither saying a word. Tyler was the first to find a smile. "Well, we should be good company for each other, then."

She said nothing. He yawned. "I guess I need some sleep," he said, massaging the back of his neck.

Amber started to leave, then realized where they were. "You're in my tent. Get out."

"Good night, Dr. Saxton," Tyler said. "Sleep well. Maybe we'll be home in the morning."

****

Tyler awoke feeling considerably rested and in good spirits. It had become customary for him to eat with the general and the other advisors and then check on Amber, who always ate a hasty breakfast before going to work with the medical staff. When they marched, Tyler caught himself taking an avid interest in the men who paid an extra amount of attention to her. These were usually the young, single soldiers, and Tyler realized he was experiencing true jealousy for the first time in his life.

He often rode back through the regiment merely to locate her and assure himself that all was well. She would smile at him and wink, never breaking her stride or conversation. He looked forward to the afternoons when she rode with him and he didn't have to worry that she would be receiving too much attention from someone else. He was just trying to keep her safe, he told himself continually, and make sure she didn't slip up and say something she shouldn't. He tried to ignore the fact that every time she so much as smiled at another man, he wanted to yank her away and stuff her in her tent.

Amber was an early riser, and the obscene morning hours didn't seem to affect her the way they did him. Knowing this, he was surprised to find her looking exhausted with dark circles under her eyes.

"What's wrong?" he asked her, concerned.

She rubbed her eyes and stifled a yawn. "I didn't sleep much last night."

"Thinking about me, were you?"

She scowled. "Why are you so cheery this morning?"

"I have no idea." He heard the call to prepare to move out. "You finish here, and I'll be back with the horse. You can ride with me this morning."

She opened her mouth to argue, but he raised his hand for silence. "You may as well save your breath. You know I'll be able to find you."

He looked back at her as he walked off to retrieve their belongings. Something was different. He studied her for a minute and then smiled. Her dress was a good four inches off the ground. If she did any more hemming, she'd be deemed unfit for proper society.

Tyler was still smiling when Major O'Brian approached and began speaking rapidly. "We don't have much time, so I'll be direct. I'd like to know what your intentions are where Dr. Saxton is concerned."

Tyler slowly stopped saddling his horse and turned to face Ian. "Why?"

"Because I've come to care for her a great deal," said Ian, "and while you're very protective of her, I'm not at all sure she needs someone like you."

"So tell me, O'Brian, who does she need?"

"She needs someone who will treat her like a lady, not a barmaid," O'Brian replied.

"You think I treat her like a barmaid?"

"Yes, quite frankly, I do," said Ian. "You snap your fingers and expect her to come running, and I don't think you realize how intelligent she is."

Tyler shook his head. "The women would love you where I'm from, O'Brian." He finished saddling the horse and mounted it. "Unfortunately for you, though, Amber is not available."

Ian looked surprised. "She never gave me the impression she was spoken for."

"Well, she is." Tyler gave him a hard look, then turned and rode to find Amber.

Tyler assumed she was still miffed about their altercation the night before when they had been riding for ten minutes and she hadn't said a word.

"I need to apologize again, I suppose," he said to her.

She looked at him, surprised. "Why?"

"For being rude last night."

She waved her hand. "Oh, that. I forgive you."

He laughed. "Well, thank you, your highness. I figured you were up all night because of me."

"You flatter yourself," she smiled. "No," she shook her head and lowered her voice. "I was up all night trying to remember what I could about the Vicksburg Campaign." She yawned. "I meant to talk to you about it after the meeting last night. Needless to say, I forgot." She gave him a sidelong glance, playfully reliving her annoyance from the night before.

He grinned, and she realized that had any true hostility remained, it would have melted away instantly. She told him what she could remember, which really wasn't more than a few minor details. "I'm afraid my concentration leaned more toward the natural sciences, not social sciences."

"It's just as well. We wouldn't want to accidentally sway the course of history, I guess."

She nodded in agreement, yawning again. They lapsed into silence, and before long she sagged wearily back against his chest. *I'll just relax for a minute*, she told herself.

He smiled when he heard her deep, even breathing and realized she was asleep. He tugged her cloak more securely about her and rested his chin on the top of her head, feeling strangely content for the first time in his life.

Chapter 15

Tyler sat in the general's tent, trying not to breathe. He strained desperately to hear the conversation being spoken in low, muted voices just behind the tent.

"What do you mean, they can't get through?" The angry tremor in the general's voice betrayed his agitation.

Tyler recognized the voice of Major Edwards in response. "The Confederate spy was caught. He was interrogated, but apparently hasn't told them anything."

General Montgomery breathed an audible sigh of relief. "There's no way they can trace it to me, then?"

"No, sir. Not unless the soldier talks," came the quiet reply.

The general was silent for a moment. "We need to be sure, then, that he is persuaded to keep quiet."

"Yes, sir. I'll take care of it."

"Where is the boy being held?" asked the general.

"In a jail just outside Vicksburg."

"Good. We'll be there soon enough."

The men moved out of Tyler's earshot, preventing him from hearing anything further. He was still sitting quietly in thought when Amber entered the tent several minutes later. She stopped abruptly when she saw him. "What are you doing?"

He looked up, his expression grim. "He's up to something," he replied quietly.

"Who? The general?"

Tyler nodded and put a finger to his lips.

"Well, I have a few minutes for lunch, and I was wondering if you'd like to join me." Tyler raised his eyebrows, stretched, and yawned. "Are you asking me out?"

Her lips twitched. "Well, such as it is, I suppose. I'm sure you've eaten in better surroundings and with more aptly dressed women, but what's a girl to do?"

He rose, grinning wickedly, and took her arm as they left the tent. "Well, I'll tell you this. I've never dated a woman wearing an authentic Civil War nurse's uniform before. Just when I thought I'd experienced everything life has to offer, you're a first." *In more ways than one*, he had to inwardly confess. The woman was becoming a drug he couldn't seem to function without. He shrugged the thought aside.

Tyler became silent and pensive throughout the bland meal and seemed distantly preoccupied. The playfulness of the moment before had vanished without a trace. Amber moved closer to where he sat and whispered, "What's he doing? Can't you tell me about it?"

"Not here," he replied absently. "We'll go for a walk later."

"Let's go now. No one's paying attention, and I may be too busy later."

He glanced casually around and stood, motioning with his head for her to join him. They had walked away from the camp in companionable silence when Tyler quietly told her what he'd overheard.

She digested the news with one eyebrow raised. "What do you think he's doing?" she finally asked.

"I have no idea," Tyler answered. "I'll see if I can find anything of interest in his desk, but I'm sure he's careful. He didn't know I was in the tent when he was talking to Edwards."

"Who?"

"Edwards. The one who always hangs around the general when everyone else is told to leave."

Amber wrinkled her nose in distaste. "Oh, him. He tried to corner me behind the medical tent the other day."

Tyler looked at her sharply. "What did he do?"

Amber hesitated.

"Well?" Tyler pressed.

"Nothing, really. He just tried to convince me that I'm as lonely as he is, and that the two of us should be lonely together," she finished with a smile. "I took care of it."

"The same way you took care of Matthews back at the hospital in D.C.?"

Amber started in surprise. "I didn't think anyone knew about that."

Tyler leaned back against a tree and folded his arms. "Boyd and I saw the entire . . . exchange."

Amber felt her patience wearing thin. "I don't understand what you want me to do. Should I scream for you every time something happens? You know, I took great pains a few years ago to learn how to defend myself, so what's your problem?"

"I don't have a problem with it. I just . . . ," Tyler began.

"You just what?"

I worry about you. I don't want anything to happen to you. I wish I could just stay with you all the time so I could defend you myself. "I just think that one of these days you won't be able to handle yourself," he finally said.

"Tyler, I can't hide from life for fear something will happen to me. I'd go insane. What if you weren't here right now? What if I were into this by myself?" She shuddered involuntarily at the thought.

He fought an absurd impulse to pull her into his arms and squeeze her. "You're not by yourself—that's my point."

She was thoughtful for a moment. "Maybe that's why we're here. You know, to find out about whatever it is the general's doing."

Tyler nodded. "I hope so. I'd like to get this over with."

"Me too," she agreed. "Could there be anything else?"

He shook his head. "I don't know. I'm driving myself crazy trying to figure everything out. How's your work with the medical team?"

"It's as good as it can be," she replied. "I'm doing what I can with what little there is. I'm frustrated, though. And edgy."

He nodded, understanding completely. He looked at her intently, the worry written clearly on his face. "Just be careful."

"I always am." She smiled softly, touched by his obvious concern.

"We'd better head back," he said, not really wanting to leave.

She nodded in agreement but didn't move. Tyler reached out and put his hand behind her neck. He pulled her close, and when she didn't resist, he leaned down and touched his lips softly to hers. She responded by clutching a fistful of his uniform with one hand and reaching up with the other to softly touch the back of his neck. She had been wanting to kiss him forever, it seemed. His arm had tightly encircled her waist, pulling her closer, and he was completely lost in the deepening kiss when he heard the general bellowing from the camp.

He pulled back reluctantly, his breathing ragged and harsh, and looked at Amber, whose eyes were cloudy and unfocused. She made a small sound of protest at the separation. He shook his head, trying to clear it, and roughly grabbed her hand. "Come on," he urged, and began a brisk pace toward the camp.

Amber stumbled and tried to keep up with him. "What are you *doing?*" she demanded, bewildered.

"I don't want him to catch us like that," he replied, tense.

"Who?"

Her question was answered as the general's voice rang out again. "Kirk! Where are you?!"

Amber watched Tyler's jaw clench in agitation. "I hate that man." He bit the words out in obvious fury, and stopped abruptly when they reached the outskirts of the camp. He quickly turned her to face him and began firing instructions in a low voice.

"Wait here for a minute until I've gone to see what he wants. Don't follow me too closely, and go to your tent or to the medical area." He glanced around quickly. "I don't want him to know we've been alone together."

"We're alone together all the time," Amber said. "I don't understand—"

"Just trust me! If he thinks we're . . . involved . . . he'll keep you away from me. Amber, he wants you for himself. He's just waiting for the time to be right." Tyler shook his head at the look of disbelief that crossed Amber's face. He squeezed her shoulders and looked intently into her face. Then he was gone.

Amber remained where she was for several minutes, completely confused. Everything had happened so fast that she couldn't seem to make sense of it. She began walking slowly toward the medical area, mentally shaking her head.

The regiment had reached Grand Junction, Tennessee uneventfully, and had been sitting idle for eleven days. During that time, Amber had observed Tyler in a variety of situations, all of which had increased her admiration for him immensely. She had seen him settle disputes, soothe tempers, answer questions, and provide general leadership that was proving to be a comfort to all those in the regiment. He trained and practiced fighting maneuvers with the soldiers, learning from them and offering suggestions of his own in preparation for the eventual battles that everyone knew were inevitable.

The more she observed him, the more Amber found herself wanting to be with Tyler. She knew that at first the attraction had been unavoidable because of the odd situation in which they had found themselves. They'd have bonded together regardless of personality similarities or differences by virtue of the fact that they were both terribly frightened and more than a little awed by the twist of fate that had them scrambling for a sense of reality.

As time progressed, however, Amber realized there was more to the attraction, on her part at least, than simple necessity. He was bright, strong, and even witty, which had caught her completely by surprise. In the weeks that had passed, he had allowed a very personable side of his character to emerge, charming all those with whom he came in contact. She would have undoubtedly found him perfect, she realized, if she didn't know that he was also extremely cynical, bitter, and had an icy temper that he barely managed to keep in check at times. She had seen the muscles in his jaw clenching as he attempted to restrain himself in conversations with the general on more than one occasion. She couldn't say she blamed him, though. The general was not a nice man.

She smiled ruefully to herself as she made her way past the general's tent toward the medical unit. She had always prided herself on her ability to be honest about her feelings, and she knew it was useless to try to convince herself she wasn't attracted to Tyler. Her breath caught at the memory of his kiss; the urgency combined with a tenderness that made her knees weak.

Amber was so consumed in her thoughts that she nearly collided with Ian O'Brian, who was walking toward her from the other direction. He reached out and caught her arms, preventing her from stumbling backward into the dirt.

"Dare I hope that smile is for me, Amber?" Ian's expression was comically hopeful.

"Ian!" she laughed. "I'm sorry. I wasn't paying attention."

He smiled. "I've been trying to find you all morning. I did a little searching, and I found a small gathering of Church members that meets weekly at the Dietrich home, which is about a mile and a half from here. I was wondering if you'd like to go with me this Sunday, provided we can get away, of course."

Her face lit up and her eyes shone. "I'd love to! You have no idea how much that would mean to me. I'm . . . a long way from home." She faltered and was silent for a moment. "I would really enjoy it. Thank you." Her smile was grateful and sincere.

Tyler stood near the general's tent, observing the entire scene but unable to hear what was being said. He cursed himself for being vulnerable enough to surrender his fragile emotions to a woman who seemed content only when every man alive groveled at her feet.

****

Amber worked late into the night and returned to her tent exhausted. Many of the soldiers in the regiment were coming down with typhoid or dysentery, largely due to the fact that their sanitary habits were deplorable. She found herself repeating the same instructions over and over again, warning of the importance of washing after using the latrine, much to the embarrassment of the men.

In addition, infection in wounds that had been improperly cared for was a problem that was nearly insurmountable. Amber did her best to keep the wounds clean and in fresh bandages, but inwardly despaired at the lack of antibiotics and modern medicine that would help so many of those she treated. She often found herself gritting her teeth in frustration because of the limited supplies, inefficient medication, and archaic mentality of the doctors and soldiers alike.

Amber opened the bag in her tent and fished out two stale biscuits and some hardtack. She carried her meager fare to the log outside her tent flap and wearily sat to watch for Tyler. She finished her meal and began to wonder if he had already gone to bed.

Amber yawned and dragged herself into her tent, too tired to wait up any longer. Despite the cold, she was asleep in seconds. She dreamed she was back at George Washington University Hospital in her own time. The halls were filled with men in Civil War uniforms, bleeding and dying. She wandered in and out of the operating rooms, unable to find any sterilized instruments or productive medicine. The wounded were reaching out to her, begging and pleading for her to save them. One man stood and grabbed her by the shoulders. He shook her until she felt her head would snap off.

"Amber, wake up. Come on, I need to talk to you." A familiar male voice broke through her dream.

Amber opened her eyes to find Tyler's face inches from her own, his hands gently shaking her shoulders. She blinked at the light of a small lantern he had brought into the tent, her heart pounding and her thoughts jumbled and cloudy. Tyler pulled her into a sitting position and searched her face for signs of coherence. "Are you awake yet?"

She forced her eyes to stay open and stifled a yawn. "What's wrong?" she mumbled sleepily.

"Nothing's wrong," he said. "I just need to tell you something."

"Tell me what?"

He took a deep breath. "We're going on a reconnaissance mission."

Her eyes snapped open wide and she stared at him. "What?"

"General Grant is sending some troops to Ripley, Mississippi, to try to see what kind of Confederate forces are defending Vicksburg. My grandfather decided to offer some additional reinforcements, so he's sending me and a few others." He paused.

"And?"

"I told him we needed at least one physician to accompany us and suggested you would be the most logical choice," Tyler said.

"Why me?"

He hesitated, not wanting to tell her the reasons he had given the general. He finally decided to be honest. "I told him that while you are physically strong and a very competent doctor, you have become emotionally dependent on me and might not fare so well in my absence."

Amber looked him in the eye for several moments before answering. "He bought that?"

"Not really, but he didn't argue with me."

"Tyler, I have work to do here. We're swamped as it is." She spoke quietly and gently. "I really don't think either of us should—"

"Amber, I'm sorry, but I have to go and there is no way I'm leaving you here. Please don't ask me to explain, because I can't. I have to go with my instincts."

"If you're trying to keep me safe, you must realize that I'm probably better off here in camp than with a handful of people off on some fact-finding mission in enemy territory."

Tyler rubbed his eyes, clearly exhausted. "Let me tell you something, Amber, that I've never told anyone." He paused again and she waited patiently. "My father was abusive, in every sense of the word. He beat my sister and my mother and me. When I got older and bigger than he was, he eventually stopped. I found out after he died that he'd sexually molested my sister. My mother couldn't cope. She was in and out of mental wards for years while I was growing up, which was a huge embarrassment for my father. She was home when I was young, but as time went on, we saw her less and less. I have, basically, no relationship at all with her anymore." His voice was flat and completely emotionless. Amber felt sick.

"The general is a mirror image of my father. He looks like him, sounds like him, and their attitudes are exactly the same." Tyler's eyes were red-rimmed and intense as he looked at Amber. "I have no doubt that he will move in on you when he feels the moment is right. He'll do whatever he has to do to keep you quiet. It won't bother him in the least that you're not a willing participant. He may even prefer it that way."

Amber closed her eyes and dropped her head, not wanting to hear any more.

"I've seen how he looks at you, Amber," he continued, his voice dropping to a barely audible whisper. "You wouldn't stand a chance. He is ruthless and clever. All the self-defense tricks in the world won't stop him. He'll catch you when you least expect it."

They sat in silence, motionless for several moments. Tyler finally spoke again. "What it boils down to is this: I know there are other men here who would watch out for you if I asked. That's not the issue."

"What is the issue, then?" Her voice was strained.

"This whole situation here, with my *grandfather*," he spat the word distastefully, "is too much like my past with my father."

Amber suddenly understood, and it made her heart ache. "You think you failed your sister, so now you're trying to make it right by protecting me?" Her voice was soft and she swallowed the lump in her throat.

Tyler clenched his jaw. "I don't think I want to talk about this anymore."

She laid a hand tentatively on his arm and felt the muscles beneath her fingers move as he tightened and released his fist. "It wasn't your fault," she insisted, horrified that he had been blaming himself for years. "You had no way of knowing."

He swore and scowled derisively at her. "Of course I should have known." He stood abruptly. "Anyway, we leave right after breakfast at six o'clock. We should be gone only a couple of days."

Amber slowly extinguished the lamp and sat alone in the darkness, her thoughts flying in a million different directions. She was finally able to mentally settle into the one notion that disturbed her the most, and she clung to it long enough to come to some sense of resolution. Tyler had been blaming himself for his sister's hellish past. If the only way he could exorcise such horrific demons was to protect Amber from the general, then she would be the last one to stand in his way. Maybe he would find some sense of peace. It was a long time before she finally fell into an exhausted and fitful slumber.

Chapter 16

Following a quick breakfast, the small group of five made its way out of camp, destined for the meeting place with General Grant's reconnaissance team. Tyler did his best to conceal his annoyance with Major Edwards, who had assumed a pseudo-command that no one in the group was inclined to follow. Edwards finally stopped trying to discuss the mission's finer points when he realized no one was paying attention to him. They'd been over the plan twice in the general's tent before they left camp. Amber, who was tied up with an overabundance of sick soldiers at the medical station, was the only member of the team who had missed the briefing. The tentative plan was to meet with General Grant's team, and upon completion of the two-day ride, they were to ascertain the size of Lee's forces surrounding Vicksburg.

The pace was rapid, and in order to keep up, Amber's horseback riding skills improved quickly. She wore the bigger of her two uniforms which, when combined with her cape, provided her with enough material to allow her to sit astride the horse and still be considered modest. They met with the five people from Grant's forces at the preappointed location without incident, and Amber and Tyler uttered the same name simultaneously upon seeing one of the men in the group: "Boyd!"

The young soldier nodded bashfully and nudged his horse forward, extending his hand. "Dr. Saxton, nice to see you again." He turned to Tyler. "Captain." He then noticed the emblem on Tyler's coat. "Excuse me, I see it's now Major. Congratulations, sir."

"Thank you, Boyd." Tyler grasped his hand in genuine friendship. "It's good to see you're doing well. What are you doing clear down here? I thought you went back to the hospital."

"I requested a transfer and took up with Grant as he traveled south," Boyd said.

"The boy's done real well," said another man, the apparent leader of the group. He rode forward and shook Tyler's hand. "I'm Lieutenant Colonel Pembroke. Boyd, here, has become my right hand."

"So we have a woman along for entertainment, huh?" one of the men leered. Tyler shot him a look so chilling that the soldier sobered instantly.

"This is Dr. Saxton," Tyler stated. "She is accompanying us at my insistence to handle any medical emergencies that may arise. You will treat her with respect."

"Yes, sir," the soldier murmured.

Pembroke apologized for the young soldier's behavior and quickly continued the introductions. "Now, that's done. Shall we be on our way?" The group turned and headed south for Ripley, Mississippi.

****

Amber adjusted her bedroll, unconsciously shifting it closer to Tyler's. The second day of the journey passed as uneventfully as had the first, and the small group set up camp at a point close enough for easy access to the Confederate camp, but far enough away to avoid detection. They had ridden hard, and Amber was exhausted and ready for some much-needed sleep.

"What I wouldn't give for a comfortable bed," she muttered to herself. She removed her dinner from her saddlebags and was munching on a hard biscuit when Tyler excused himself from Pembroke and approached her, his hands in his pockets and one eyebrow raised.

"After all the meals I've prepared for you, not only do you not get my food ready, but you eat without me?"

She grinned and took another bite. "You'll have to excuse my lack of domestic courtesy. I'm used to looking out for myself."

"So am I."

"You must be more inherently thoughtful than I am."

"Yeah, whatever." He retrieved his own food from his saddlebags and joined her on the ground.

Several hours later, Amber tossed and turned in her bedroll, unable to stay asleep for more than a few minutes at a time. She opened her eyes and tried to orient herself. The sky was dark, the light from the moon completely obliterated by clouds that shifted and rumbled, and allowed only sparse illumination from a few stars to break through to the ground below.

She was sick of being cold. She hadn't seen the inside of a warmly lit building for weeks. While the regiment had indeed been marching south, and she was grateful to avoid the snow she knew was covering the ground in D.C., it was still cold in the southern states, especially at night. She had made a habit of putting on every pair of socks she owned, and she thanked the stars above that she had been wearing thermals under her scrub suit when she had changed for work at George Washington that ill-fated afternoon.

Amber rubbed her eyes, glanced over at Tyler's bedroll, and was startled to find it empty. She sat up and scanned the area, finally locating him sitting alone on a log on the outskirts of the campsite. She rose, and pulling her cape around her shoulders, she approached Tyler and sat next to him on the log. "Can't sleep?"

He glanced at her and offered a half-hearted smile. "Neither can you, I see."

"What are you thinking about, here by yourself?"

Tyler shrugged. "Nothing and everything, I guess."

Amber glanced down at the bottle he held suspended loosely between two fingers. She was surprised. She'd never seen him drink. "What are you doing with that?" she asked, gesturing toward the bottle.

"Well, we can't all be as disciplined as you, now can we, Dr. Saxton?"

She realized he'd had quite a bit as she looked closely at his face. His speech wasn't slurred, but his eyes were unnaturally bright and even in the dim light she noticed his face was flushed. She gave a low, involuntary laugh and shook her head.

"What's so funny?" he wanted to know.

"You're never out of control," she told him. "Not even when you're drunk."

"I'm not drunk." He continued staring into the darkness. The clouds overhead shifted, revealing a full moon that cast its light downward, offering Amber a view of Tyler's profile. She couldn't help staring at his chiseled features; the straight nose, the full mouth. It had been a while since his last haircut, and the extra growth was a contradiction to his impeccably neat personality. She reacted impulsively and gently ran her fingers through his hair above his ear, combing it up and back.

Tyler shot her a wry glance. "Careful, Amber. My head isn't too clear, and I wouldn't want to do something I'd regret in the morning."

She dropped her hand, but smiled. "Come on, Tyler," she said softly. "I can't picture you being the cause of the damsel's distress."

"Just keep your hands to yourself."

She felt a little foolish. "So what has you so upset that you'd sneak away in the middle of the night with a bottle of whiskey?"

He was quiet for so long she thought he was ignoring her. "Life," he finally muttered.

"You mean lately, or in general?"

He shrugged. "I finally escaped from one madman, only to be thrown into the company of another who might as well be the same man."

She was thoughtful. "I miss my old life. I miss Liz, my sister. I miss my job. I miss Camille." She laughed. "I even miss my dad's Aunt Lucy. You know, she's the kind that makes family dinners really interesting. She's one of those weird relatives that every family has."

"Yeah. Mine were called parents."

Amber paused, then continued, determined to keep the conversation light. "I miss my parents, too. It's frustrating, knowing that I can't just jump on a plane and be with them in a few hours." She smiled ruefully. "Right now, the Salt Lake Airport is one big desert."

He looked at her sharply. "I thought you were from Seattle."

"I never said I was," she said. "That whole story was, well, just a story. I'm from Utah."

He was thoughtful. "I lived in Ogden until the end of fifth grade."

She started in surprise. "Wow! What a small world. I grew up in Ogden. My parents still live there."

He told her his former address and she nearly choked. "We must have gone to the same elementary school!"

"What an amazing coincidence."

"It is!" she exclaimed with conviction. "Aren't you a little surprised?"

"Disgusted, actually," Tyler said. "The last thing I need is another reminder of my childhood."

Amber remained silent.

"You said you were a Mormon," Tyler muttered more to himself than to her. "I ought to have guessed."

"Hey!" she said, finally annoyed. "Just because your father was an abusive bigot doesn't mean we all are, so quit trying to shove everyone into your nice, neat little molds."

"Oh, come on, Amber," Tyler shot back. "It exists in all degrees. How many non-white people did your parents have over for dinner?"

She glared at him. "My best friend is an African-American. Our parents are good friends. We were at each other's house all the time."

He snorted. "I bet you have no idea where she is today."

"Well, assuming she hasn't been sucked into some wacky wormhole the way we've been, she's probably back in D.C., either in our apartment or at work," said Amber.

He was silent for a moment, staring blankly at her face.

"Yes, she's Camille, my college roommate," Amber continued. "She came to George Washington when she finished high school, and we've been roommates ever since. She just finished her M.B.A."

Amber was silent for a moment, trying to calm herself. She sighed. "Not that you deserve an explanation, but Camille stuck by me when everyone else thought I was weird," she said. "I had just started medical school when she came to D.C." She smiled. "What a relief she was to me. She understood me like no one else. She's very nurturing—the kind of person who knows how to truly care for others." Amber paused. "She got mad at our friends who pressured me to drink. She defended my morality standards. She didn't have to. She wasn't LDS until two years ago."

Tyler raised his eyebrows. "If she's so wonderful, maybe you should forget men altogether and marry her."

Amber scowled at him. "You are drunk." She suddenly laughed. "She does have a brother, actually. About your age, I would guess. I had the biggest crush on him, and he always thought I was such an irritant."

She shook her head at the memory. "I remember when they first moved to the neighborhood, Camille and I were playing at recess and some third-grader took our foursquare ball. We ran and found Jared, Camille's brother, and his new friend. They scared the bully and made him give the ball back." She laughed again. "I was a gutsy kid; either that or really stupid. I yelled at the third-grader for saying girls couldn't play ball like boys could."

Tyler slowly pieced together the bits of information she was giving him. "What did you say his name was?" he asked, his voice barely audible.

"Whose?"

"Camille's brother," Tyler clarified.

"Jared."

"Jared," he repeated. "I knew him." His eyes misted and his throat hurt. Amber was silent. "He was actually the reason we moved."

"What?"

"My parents found out we were friends, and my father was disgusted," Tyler began. "He had been debating whether or not to take an out-of-state transfer. He found out I went to Jared's house one day after school, and that was it. We moved to Boston, and I was sent to a very WASP-ish school for boys."

Amber was at a loss for words. "I'm so sorry," she finally said. "When we get back home," *if we get back home*, "I'll give you his phone number. He'd love to hear from you, I'm sure. He lives in Portland now. He's an architect."

They were silent for a while, Tyler consumed in his own thoughts and Amber searching for a way to learn more about him without arousing his temper.

"So your father was a Mormon?" she finally asked.

"Yes," Tyler reluctantly admitted. "He wasn't a very committed member, though. He thought they were all idiots. I think my friendship with Jared was a convenient excuse for him to leave the state. The only friends I ever associated with outside of school were kids of my father's choosing. There wasn't a Mormon among them. I didn't actually have many friends at all until I got older."

"So who would you say you connected with as a child?" she asked. "Any adult influence at all?"

Tyler rubbed his eyes. "My mom was good for me when I was younger. When she was home." His expression softened at the memory. "She always loved me. I never doubted that. She just wasn't strong enough to take care of herself and us, too." He was quiet for a minute. "I had a Scout leader, too, that I was closer to than anyone. He was a really good man." Tyler thought of the times throughout the years that he'd reflected on his friendship with his former Scout leader and smiled. "I used to wish he was my father."

"Hmmm. Imagine that." Amber couldn't keep the sarcasm from dripping off each word. "A Scout leader in Utah, huh? He was probably LDS then, wasn't he? Well, what do you know. We're not all rotten."

Tyler stared at her. "I never said you were all rotten. And come to think of it, he probably was LDS. We had activities at the church, but all Scouting activities in Utah took place at the LDS churches. I didn't necessarily connect the two—we never talked about anything religious." He snorted. "My father must not have known my Scout leader was a Mormon. Once again, I get the last laugh."

"You've had the last laugh before?"

"Yeah," Tyler said. "I outlived him and have nothing to do with anything he liked."

Amber tried for a different topic. "So why have you never married?"

"What, and repeat history?" He looked disgusted.

"What do you mean?"

He shook his head. "I don't want to be like my father."

"Tyler, if your father was really as much like the general as you say, then you have nothing to worry about," Amber offered quietly. "The only similarities are physical."

Tyler rubbed his eyes and took another drink from the bottle. "It's in the genes. People who were abused will most likely abuse. Surely you've had a psych class or two."

Amber smiled. "You're a smart man, Tyler. You must realize that the cycle can be broken."

When he made no reply, she tried a different approach. "I assume you've had a couple of girlfriends in your life?"

He eyed her warily. "Yes."

"Did any of them ever make you mad?"

"What's your point?" His irritation was evident.

"Did you ever hit any of them, or hurt them?"

He rolled his eyes at her.

"Answer me honestly," she said.

"No. I have never struck a woman."

Amber took his hand and held it between her own. "Look at me."

He reluctantly looked into her green eyes, which seemed to glow in the darkness.

"I cannot picture you ever being cruel," she said. "Not to people you care about."

He looked grim. "You can see me being cruel, though."

"To someone unjust or mean, yes. In order to defend those who can't defend themselves. And even then I wouldn't call it cruelty. I'd call it just." She smiled. "I've seen shades of that temper."

He looked worn and exhausted. "Yeah, well, sometimes the best of intentions go astray."

Amber gave his hand a squeeze. "So you have a temper! Big deal. So does my dad. So do I, for that matter." No response. She continued, desperately. "Don't you know how much I've come to depend on your company? I trust you with my life," she softly confessed. "You'd make a wonderful husband and father."

His gaze wandered over her beautiful face, softly illuminated by the moonlight. She had the most innocent and sincere-looking eyes he'd ever seen. "You almost make me believe it's possible," he murmured.

"Well, of course it is."

He set the bottle down. Taking her face between his hands, he gently pushed her hair out of her eyes and ran his finger down the side of her face and along the line of her jaw. She closed her eyes as he traced her eyebrows and eyelids, his finger trailing down her nose and finally coming to rest on her lips.

Amber opened her eyes to see Tyler's face inches from her own. "You are so beautiful," she heard him whisper. She closed her eyes again as he put his hand behind her neck and pulled her to his lips.

He kissed her with all the pent-up emotion he'd felt for years. His tongue traced her lips, and she groaned as she felt his hand slide slowly downward from her neck. *I have to stop this now*, she heard herself think. She shoved the pesky inner voice aside.

Amber finally snapped back into reality when she realized that Tyler had no intention of stopping either. She didn't want him to. That was the problem.

"Tyler, wait," she said, pushing on his chest. He lifted his head, his eyes cloudy and unfocused. She bit her lip and ran a hand nervously through her hair. "I've been through all this before. I can't do it again."

He looked at her as though he couldn't comprehend what she was saying.

"Please understand, it isn't that I don't want to . . ." Her voice trailed off.

The fog in his brain finally seemed to clear, and he dropped his hands. "What do you want from me, Amber?" His voice was flat.

"I don't know." The despair was evident on her face. "I just know that I can't go through that whole mess a second time."

"Mess? What mess?"

"Don't you remember me telling you about my boyfriend who I had some . . . morality problems with?"

His eyes narrowed. "You're comparing me to an old boyfriend?"

"No!" She paused in frustration. "I don't know how to make you understand what a big deal it is to Mormons to avoid, well, situations that could lead to, well . . ."

"You're not a little girl anymore, Amber," Tyler said. "Your mommy and daddy are nowhere to be found. What are you afraid of?"

"I'm not afraid of anything. I just have some very strong convictions."

Tyler rubbed a shaking hand on the back of his neck in an effort to ease his tension. "You're a smart woman, I know that firsthand," he finally said. "How can you let a religion run your life?"

"Because I know in my heart it's true. I've had too many prayers answered to deny it. I know what's right and what isn't. If I'm going to lay claim to possessing any amount of integrity in this life, I have to make a stand. I can't just pick and choose the counsel I'm going to follow." Her voice faltered. "I don't know what else to say. I just feel good when I live by my church standards." She shrugged miserably, looking anything but content.

Had he been sober and the situation less emotionally charged, he might have laughed at the contradiction between her words and her demeanor. He looked into her face with such intensity her heart raced. "I can make you feel good, Amber."

She nearly groaned. "I don't doubt it," she whispered honestly. "But that's only temporary. Sooner or later I would feel the guilt. I've been through it before, and it's wretched."

Amber felt the tears escape and slip down her cheeks. "You have no idea how hard this is for me to do. I've come to care for you so much. I think I—"

Tyler put a finger to her lips. "Don't say it."

Great. I'm finally with a man I genuinely love, and he doesn't want to hear about it.

She put her face in her hands and braced her elbows on her knees. Tyler moved close and rested his hand on her back, rubbing comfortingly back and forth as she tried to control her tears.

In the days and weeks prior, he'd seen her angry, frustrated, and tired, but he hadn't seen her weep since the first night at the hospital in D.C., and he found it unsettling. "Don't cry anymore, Amber. I'll respect your religion. From now on we'll just shake hands."

She laughed and sat up, wiping her face on the handkerchief he held out to her. "I'm so tired," she said, her voice muffled as she wiped her nose. "I want my own bed."

Tyler refrained from making a lewd comment about the fact that he wanted her bed, too. Instead, he gave her shoulders a squeeze and said, "You go on back to sleep. I'll be there in a minute." He pulled her close and kissed her forehead.

She smiled, and putting her hands on either side of his face, she kissed his lips softly. Then she stood and walked slowly back to camp.

I love you too, Amber, Tyler thought to himself as he watched her retreating form. He hadn't actually said those words aloud since his childhood, when he'd felt close to his mother. What a calming sensation it was, to realize that he loved her. It was calming and frightening at the same time. It caught him by surprise. It meant he was giving her the power to hurt him. He watched her attempt to settle down for the remainder of the night and smiled despite his earlier frustration. He thought back on the things she had said to him, and in his heart he granted her something he had never thought he would truly give to anyone. His respect.

Chapter 17

The morning dawned much earlier than Amber would have liked. She sat up and looked around, trying to remember where she was. Her eyes were half closed and her hair fell in wild disarray around her shoulders.

Tyler glanced at the other men who were all looking as though they'd like to devour her whole. He placed his hand firmly under her elbow and helped her to rise. "Come on, Doctor. I'll stand guard over there in those trees so you can do whatever it is you may need to do."

She looked at him in confusion as she rose.

"You need to put up your hair, too. I'm afraid you're looking a bit too modern," he muttered as they walked. "I'd hate to have to fight every man here."

She smiled sleepily. "You'd do that for me?"

"Don't let it go to your head. It's too big as it is."

They had reached the edge of a thick copse of trees. She scowled at him and marched on ahead. "Don't you have a hangover or something?"

He winced. "Not so loud, please."

She smirked and hastily took care of her bodily functions. Never again, she decided, would she take a toilet for granted. Or a shower, for that matter. She'd had enough spit-baths now to last a lifetime, and had given herself massive headaches by washing her hair in streams that were nigh unto freezing. She emerged from the trees to find Tyler rubbing his eyes and groaning. "What's wrong?" she asked.

"Nothing," he said.

"A little bloodshot, are we?"

"Be quiet, Amber."

The men had cleared their bedrolls and were eating breakfast when Amber and Tyler returned to camp. Pembroke was speaking to the group. "You all have your Confederate uniforms, I assume?" The men all nodded and turned to their saddlebags to retrieve them.

Amber turned to her own bags and pulled out a plain, blue print dress, an armful of fluffy petticoats, and an apron. Tyler noticed her actions and pulled her away from the others. "What do you think you're doing?" he asked without preamble.

"I'm getting ready to go. What does it look like?"

"Oh, no, no, no," Tyler told her. "You're staying right here. We're far enough from the base that you'll be safe. There's no way you're going into that camp. I'm sorry if I gave you the wrong impression."

She eyed him evenly. "This whole thing was your idea. I'm here because *you* insisted. I am not staying here. I'm going in, and I'll pose as a volunteer civilian nurse."

"Amber, this is ridiculous," Tyler said, his voice rising. "You'll attract too much attention."

"I will not," she argued back. "I know exactly what I'm doing."

They were interrupted by Pembroke. "Hey, you two, we have to get going. Go change your clothes."

Amber glared at Tyler in triumph and quickly disappeared into the trees. Tyler swore under his breath and began removing his clothes in such haste that he nearly tore all the buttons off his shirt.

Pinning her hair into a neat twist at the back of her head as she walked, Amber returned to the clearing looking every inch a middle-class southerner. Pembroke approached her. "Dr. Saxton, I'm not sure what your instructions were, but I have some suggestions. May I?"

Amber nodded and watched carefully as the lieutenant colonel showed her a crude sketch of the Confederate camp layout. He pointed to an area on the outskirts of the camp and told her to get an average accounting of men in uniform.

Pembroke finished with Amber's instructions and moved on to the next man. Tyler approached her, seething. "This is not what I had in mind, Amber!"

"Don't be a caveman, Major. I'm not going to be accosted in broad daylight with hundreds of other people around." Amber stuffed her regular uniform hastily into her saddlebags and swung up onto the back of the horse. She took the reins into her hands and grinned down at Tyler.

"Where did you get that dress?" he asked, eyeing the form-fitting bodice and scooped neckline.

"The general."

"Of course." Tyler stormed to his own horse and mounted.

"Major?"

Tyler turned at the sound of Amber's voice. "Yes?"

"You look good in either uniform."

"Of course I do." He waited for her to pass him and join the others before he followed, staying behind her and trying to come up with a last-minute plan to make her abandon her absurd plan. His mind was blank.

It wasn't until later that Amber realized the significance of the fact that Tyler was wearing a Confederate uniform. He'd been wearing just such a uniform when she had seen him in the hospital . . . with the gunshot wound.

****

Amber walked casually toward her designated area, taking in the sights and sounds of the Confederate camp and trying to shut out the image of Tyler lying on an ER table, unconscious. *So this is the enemy*, she thought to herself. It didn't take long to realize that the camp was not unlike her own. The loss of life, she knew, would be staggering before the conflict was over, and she felt a sense of despair at her own helplessness.

She walked the perimeter and made a mental count of the men in uniform, attracting little attention. Carrying a roll of bandages and some bedding, she coughed profusely when anyone seemed inclined to approach her.

The group had agreed to leave separately and meet at their own little encampment when they finished. Amber had just completed her assignment and was mounting her horse, which was several hundred yards away from the Confederate camp, when she noticed Major Edwards. He had mounted his horse and was riding as fast as he could in the direction exactly opposite of the reconnaissance team encampment.

Amber was torn between her desire to be sure Tyler changed his uniform, as though such action could prevent him from getting shot, and her curiosity about the sly major's activities. Finally reasoning that Tyler would take care of himself, she urged her horse in the same direction the major had taken and followed him at a discreet distance for nearly two miles before Edwards stopped at a secluded spot near a small stream. The undergrowth was thick and Amber was hard-pressed not to make a sound as she approached the major on foot, having tied her horse to a tree several yards back and off to one side so it was hidden in the thick foliage.

She lay flat under a particularly thick group of bushes and peered out to see Edwards, who was speaking to another man, also in a Confederate uniform but not someone she recognized from the reconnaissance team.

"So, what's the new plan, then?" Edwards was saying.

"It will take a little while," the man said. "We're still looking for a new informant."

"What would you like me to tell the general then, Hawk?" Edwards was clearly agitated. "He loses money on delays like these."

"We lose money too, Edwards." The man addressed as Hawk spoke evenly. "General Morris is hosting a ball in three weeks. We'll know by then. Send a messenger—someone unsuspecting and inno-cent-looking." He handed Edwards a packet. "This is an invitation to the party and instructions on when to expect the escort."

Edwards nodded absently, taking the packet and stuffing it into his shirt. His eyes darted around nervously. "I need to go. Someone will miss me."

Amber felt the hair on the back of her neck rise and tried to turn discreetly to see behind her. Before she could do so, a hand clamped over her mouth and she was pinned down by something heavy. She felt a moment of panic before a reassuring voice sounded in her ear.

"It's me." Tyler slowly released his hand from her mouth and eased down on the ground next to her. She made a small gesture toward Edwards and his companion and turned her attention back to the pair.

The Confederate soldier was looking in the general direction of Amber and Tyler's hiding place. "Are you sure no one saw you leave?"

"Positive. I waited until everyone had left but that woman," Edwards replied testily.

"What woman?" Hawk questioned.

"She's a doctor, and Kirk insisted on bringing her." Edwards glanced about uncertainly.

"Who's Kirk?"

"A nuisance." Edwards was vehement. "The general made him his personal assistant. I can't imagine why. He hasn't told him what we're doing. He says Kirk reminds him of someone, and he keeps him around."

"Will he be a problem?"

"I don't know," said Edwards. "Possibly. He thinks highly of himself."

Amber stole a sidelong glance at Tyler, who raised his eyebrows, the corner of his mouth turned up in an obvious smirk.

"Do we need to get rid of him?" Hawk asked, his voice calm and detached.

Edwards looked queasy. "No. Not yet, anyway. I'll keep an eye on him."

Hawk again glanced at the bushes where Amber and Tyler were hidden. "I could have sworn . . . ," Amber heard him say under his breath, and she watched in horror as he advanced toward them. She glanced at Tyler, whose face was set in grim lines, his muscles bunched beneath the gray suit as though ready to spring into battle. That uniform. Was this to be the end, then? Before they had even discovered the reason they were there? As much as she had longed for home, it didn't seem right.

"Hawk!" Major Edwards was calling to the man. "Walk with me to my horse; I need to ask you a few more questions."

With a backward glance at the bushes, Hawk turned toward Edwards with a sigh of annoyance. "I've told you everything I know . . ." His voice trailed off as the men left the area.

Amber and Tyler remained where they were until the last sounds of the horses' hooves faded into the distance. Tyler stood and yanked Amber up by the shoulders.

"Are you insane?" His hands tightened their already fierce grip, and he looked angrier than Amber had ever seen him. "What were you thinking? You weren't thinking!"

Amber scowled. "I was very careful. He had no idea I'd followed him. He looked too, I don't know, shifty, I guess. I wanted to see what he was up to. Now we know it's obviously something big."

Tyler released her shoulders and grabbed his own head. "I will never understand you," he nearly shouted in frustration as he began pacing back and forth before her. "Do you think that because you've had a few self-defense classes you're invincible?"

"Come on, Tyler. I made sure I was quiet. I was very careful," she repeated.

"Not careful enough! You had no idea I was behind you. I could have been anyone!" He began to walk through the trees toward his horse and she followed him. He stopped abruptly and turned on her. "No more of this, Amber. I mean it—no more. I want you to stay away from anything the least bit suspicious. I have a lot on my mind, and I can't be constantly worried about whether or not you're off doing something stupid." He began walking briskly again.

Amber ran to catch him. "Listen, mister. You're not the only one with a lot on his mind! Besides that, I lived my own life by myself before we got stuck here, and I've been making my own decisions for a long time. I don't need your permission to do anything." Her eyes blazed. "You're no more invincible than I am. Especially wearing that uniform!"

Tyler stopped walking and grabbed her arms, shaking her. "Don't you get it? I can't believe you don't understand why I'm so mad!" He pulled her to his chest and drew his arms tightly around her back, pinning her own arms to her sides. He rested his chin on top of her head and closed his eyes in frustration.

Amber was silent, listening to Tyler's harsh breathing and contemplating the meaning of his words. "I'm sorry you were so worried," she finally whispered. "Your uniform . . ."

"What about it?"

"I want you to change out of it. It's making me nervous."

Tyler sighed and finally released her. "Great. I'd forgotten that little detail." He took her hand and led her to the horses in silence.

Chapter 18

The trip back to Grand Junction was uneventful. The small team of spies had obtained the information they were seeking, and the whole group seemed relieved to be retreating back to familiar territory.

"I never thought I'd be happy to see this cramped little tent," Amber remarked upon reaching camp. She dumped her belongings unceremoniously inside. "I'll be at the medical station if you need me," she called over her shoulder to Tyler.

He smiled grimly at her retreating form. He knew she was tired, cold, and hungry. He wished he could buy her some new clothes and take her to dinner at a nice restaurant somewhere. With resignation, he deposited his belongings in his own tent, saw to his and Amber's horses, and walked wearily to the general's tent to report on the success of the mission.

****

Dr. Davis beamed when he saw Amber. The small group of physicians and assistants looked haggard and exhausted. Amber raised her eyebrows and put her hands on her hips. "What on earth happened to all of you?"

"We've missed you, Amber," Davis laughed, clasping her hand. "This is the longest rest we've had since you left."

"What happened?" she repeated.

He sighed. "About half of us were called away to help the New York Fifth Infantry about five miles out. They were caught in a skirmish and lost most of their medical team. The other half were kept busy here. The typhoid is still spreading, and everyone else is coughing."

"So I picked an inopportune time to be gone, I assume." She turned a sympathetic eye on her colleagues. "I'll stay here through the night. You all get some rest." Some of the men were already sleeping where they sat.

"Come now, Amber," Davis replied. "You've been on a horse all day yourself."

"I'm fine, James." She smiled. "I'm used to being on call for twenty-four hour stretches." He blinked.

"Never mind," she said, patting his back. "You just go to bed."

"Well, we'll all be close by. Please find me if it becomes unmanageable." He seemed grateful that Amber was insisting. She eventually shooed the other men off to their own tents and sat down wearily on an overturned barrel. She turned a dismal eye toward the darkening countryside around her and said aloud, "I want to be done with this. I want to go home."

She wasn't sure how long she'd been staring into the darkness when she felt someone standing near her. She turned her head to see Ian smiling down at her.

"Welcome back, Amber," he said. "We all missed you."

Her face softened and a small, gentle smile played at the corners of her lips. It took Ian a moment to realize she wasn't looking at him, but to a point beyond his shoulder. He turned to find Tyler standing behind him with a tray of steaming food in his hands.

"Inside," Tyler quietly ordered Amber and inclined his head toward the medical tent. He looked at Ian as he would a pesky fly. "You can come too, if you want."

Amber lit the lantern inside the tent and motioned Tyler toward a small table. He cleared away the instruments that were stacked in boxes on the table and placed the tray before Amber. They each drew up a chair or crate and sat down.

Amber's eyes widened at the delicious aroma. She glanced at Tyler. "Where on earth did you find stew?"

"The general sends his regards."

She picked up the steaming mug and sniffed, her eyebrows drawn in confusion.

"Herbal tea," came Tyler's reply. "I took great pains to find something warm that your religion would allow you to drink."

She laughed and smiled her thanks, taking a cautious sip.

Ian cleared his throat, calling attention to himself. Amber glanced guiltily at him. "Thank you, Ian, for coming to welcome me back." She smiled. He was a good friend. The last thing she wanted to do was offend him.

Ian smiled in return. "I wanted to let you know that I've obtained permission for us to attend the church service tomorrow at the Dietrichs'. I was hoping you'd still be interested."

Amber's eyes lit up. "Absolutely!" She turned to Tyler. "Will you come with us?"

Her invitation was timely, as Tyler had just opened his mouth to insist he go along. "Yes, I'd like to."

They sat in comfortable silence while Amber did her best to tactfully devour her dinner. As she finished, Ian rose. "I should be going," he said, looking at Tyler and clearly expecting him to do likewise.

Amber choked back a horrified laugh at Tyler's nearly imperceptible nod. When Tyler made no attempt to leave, Ian cleared his throat. "Major, may I speak to you outside?"

"Certainly."

They stepped out into the brisk wind, leaving Amber to quietly sip her tea and ponder the oddities of manly rituals. Outside, Ian whirled on Tyler, who held up his hand before the tirade could even begin. "O'Brian, I know what you're going to say, and for Amber's sake, I appreciate it. But let me explain something." Tyler took a deep breath and sighed.

"Amber is a very long way from home—you have no idea just how far. Where she comes from, men and women often spend time together without a chaperone. It is a common occurrence, and one that she is used to. She enjoys my company, and if she didn't, I'm sure she would insist that I leave, in which case I certainly would."

Ian's jaw was clenched. "It's not her intentions I'm concerned about."

Tyler's expression was one of irritated disbelief. "Do you honestly think I would harm Amber or her reputation in any way?"

The two men stood in charged silence for a moment before Ian finally spoke. "If I find that you have distressed her in the least, Major, in the least—"

"I understand."

"Good." Ian reluctantly offered his hand, which Tyler took in surprise. O'Brian turned on his heel and left.

Amber looked up as Tyler entered the tent, a bemused smile on his face. "What was that all about?" she asked.

He shook his head and sat down at the table. "I feel like a chastened schoolboy. I haven't felt like this since April Beaty's father threatened me at gunpoint to have his daughter home by ten."

Amber shot him a frosty glance. "Who's April Beaty?"

Tyler smiled and reached for her hand. "No one of consequence." He kissed her fingertips.

"Humph," she said into her tea and scowled. Jealousy was not a feeling she was accustomed to. The thought of Tyler spending time with another woman made her stomach clench.

"Not a fun emotion, is it?" He gently pressed her hand between both of his and rubbed back and forth.

"I don't know what you're talking about."

"Uh-huh." He couldn't contain his delight over her reaction. She scowled at his grinning mouth.

"Stop gloating. It doesn't become you," she snapped.

"Yes ma'am," he smirked. "Like you haven't seen me jealous. How about your friend *Ian*." He sneered the last. "What kind of name is 'Ian' anyway? It's the kind of name whose butt I'd have kicked in high school, that's what. Pampered rich kid who gets everything handed to him, that's what kind of name it is . . ." Tyler trailed off at the last and muttered something unintelligible, his mockery of Amber's jealousy having faded in the face of his own.

Amber bit the insides of her cheeks to keep from laughing outright and refrained from reminding him that he had been a rich kid himself. That, plus the fact that Ian was every bit as broad through the shoulders as Tyler was, made his "butt kicking" argument a little hard to swallow. Had the two come to blows, Amber was under the impression that Tyler might well have met his match. "I had assumed from your earlier 'discussion' with him that you'd called a truce."

"Whatever." He scowled and she laughed out loud. "He's nice enough, I guess."

Amber nodded. "Yes, he is. I wish him the best." They were quiet for a moment. "I'm not a possessive person," she finally said. She reflected on the time they'd spent together and the circumstances surrounding the fact that they were together at all. She gave a short, humorless laugh. "As if I have anything to be possessive of."

"Meaning me, I assume?"

She blushed and he laughed softly.

"Really, Amber," he said. "You know you have me wrapped around your little finger."

She looked genuinely surprised.

He raised his eyebrows. "You mean you haven't noticed me following you around like an adolescent with hyperactive hormones?"

She laughed and sipped the rest of her tea. An amused expression crossing her face, she set the mug on the table. "You'd be following me around if I were eighty years old, you know, just because we're both trying to get home."

Tyler shook his head in amazement. "Amber, look at me."

Feeling foolish and vulnerable, she raised her eyes.

"How can I not be attracted to you? You're beautiful, you're smart, you're tough, you're talented—" he began.

"I'm the only woman around for miles."

Tyler released her hand and sat back in his chair with an exasperated sigh. "Let me tell you something. I have dated every type of woman in existence, from women with advanced degrees to women who have modeled in Paris and New York. I never pursued anything beyond sex." His eyes bored into hers as though he would look into her soul.

"I had never met a woman I truly wanted to converse with until I met you. I find myself wanting your opinions on everything. I want to know how you feel. I want to see you smile. You make me laugh." He took a deep breath and ran a hand through his hair. "You make me wish I'd never been with any other woman. I don't feel worthy of you, but I don't want anyone else to have you, either," he finished quietly.

He gazed at a spot beyond Amber's head, looking as vulnerable as Amber had felt. She sat in stunned silence, knowing what his confession had cost him. He was not an open person.

"I'm not perfect, you know." She leaned forward and rested her elbows on the table. "I know what regret feels like. I've done plenty of things I wish I hadn't."

"Overdue video rentals don't count."

"Oh, come on!" She laughed and was relieved to see his face relax into a smile. "I just enjoy being with you. I hate to think that I don't make you feel good about yourself."

"It's not that." He looked weary. "I don't have too many happy memories. I haven't found much to laugh at, and I've made a habit of surrounding myself with people who are as cynical as I am. When I'm with you, I feel like a devil trying to seduce an angel."

He looked so morose she couldn't help but laugh again. "Tyler, I'm not an angel, and I can't really think of too many times when you've tried to seduce me."

"I must be losing my touch." He allowed himself a small smile.

"Well, I do have a lot of happy memories. In fact," she stood up, "many of them include the time I've spent with you."

"You're kidding."

"Nope. Would you care to dance?"

"What?"

She stood before him and extended her hand. "By my best calculations, if we were at home right now, I'd be attending a charity ball for the hospital. It includes dinner and dancing. Dinner is obviously over now, so . . ."

He smiled and took her hand. Rising from the chair, he said, "Dr. Saxton, I would be honored." He bowed over her hand and kissed her fingertips.

Amber stifled a contented sigh as Tyler's right arm came around her waist and gently pulled her close. He took her right hand in his left and she placed her left hand on his shoulder. She rested her head gently against his chest and they moved slowly together in comfortable silence.

"What are you thinking?" he whispered, his cheek resting against the top of her head.

I'm thinking I could stay like this forever. I'm wishing we were home again together. I'm wondering how I'll convince you to take the missionary discussions, because I love you with all my heart. "Nothing much."

Tyler closed his eyes. "You don't really think I'm going to let you go once we get home, do you?"

His softly spoken statement left her feeling weak. She was grateful for the solid comfort of his chest and arms that kept her from collapsing into a puddle of mush. She inhaled deeply, her senses filled with his presence, and found herself scrambling for coherent thought. She had to bite her tongue to keep from swearing when she heard coughing outside the tent.

"Doctor?" Amber heard an unfamiliar man's voice.

Amber reluctantly moved to the tent flap and opened it to a handful of shivering soldiers. "Yes?"

"Sorry to bother you, ma'am. We aren't feeling too good." The soldier who had called to her spoke for himself and the rest of the sick men who nodded miserably in agreement.

She smiled. "I can see that. Come on in."

From that moment on, Amber received a steady stream of sick soldiers throughout the night. Tyler insisted on staying with her and dozed periodically on a cot in the corner. Several times as Amber was treating her patients, she glanced up to see Tyler gazing at her steadily. She winked when she caught him and he smiled in return. It was a long night.

Chapter 19

"Are you sure you want to do this?" Tyler asked Amber over breakfast. "God probably understands you're tired."

"I'm sure," Amber yawned and stuffed a biscuit into her mouth. "I've been looking forward to this. It's an opportunity of a lifetime."

It wasn't long before Ian approached, leading two horses. Tyler stood, took the reins of one, and began to mount.

"Where's mine?" Amber asked.

"You're riding with me." Tyler reached down to pull her up. "You can sleep on the way," he said when he saw she meant to argue.

"Yeah, right," she grumbled and tried to situate herself comfortably. "I'd be better off on my own horse."

"Amber, you'd fall off. Now be quiet." He shoved her head back against his chest and pulled her cloak tightly around her shoulders and under her chin.

"You didn't get much sleep last night either," she muttered.

"I got more than you did."

****

"She looks so peaceful, I hate to wake her."

As he secured his own horse to a tree, Ian glanced up at Tyler with a half-smile, the two men having decided without verbalization to call a truce. "She'll not look so peaceful anymore if she wakes up and finds out you let her sleep through the service. Besides, there's no way you could get her off that horse without waking her."

"Are you kidding? I could push her off from here and she'd stay asleep." Tyler grinned at Ian's laughter and gently rubbed Amber's arms. "Amber, wake up. We're here."

Amber's head ached as though her skull had been split in half and her eyelids felt like sandpaper. She managed to clear the clouds from her thoughts by the time the trio reached the front door of the quaint log home.

"The Dietrichs are good people," Ian said, knocking on the door. "I met them once—"

The door was flung open by a buxom woman with steel-gray hair that was pulled back into a bun. "Velcome to our home!" she boomed, smiling.

The hour that followed contained moments that Amber wanted to lock away in her heart to cherish forever. The service involved the Dietrichs and two neighboring families who stayed behind when the rest of the Saints moved west. The small group partook of the sacrament and sang hymns so dear and familiar to Amber that her throat ached with unshed tears. They listened to a brief sermon on faith, delivered by Brother Dietrich, and quietly took turns bearing testimony of the gospel. Amber was relieved to see Tyler's demeanor change as the meeting progressed. He relaxed visibly, and on his face was an expression of quiet contemplation.

Brother Dietrich asked Amber toward the end of the service if she had anything to add. She nodded. "If you don't mind," she said, "I'd like to sing something for you." The room was silent as Amber stood. She cleared her throat. "This song is one that has been of great comfort to me in my life." *Forgive me, Elder McConkie,* she thought with a wry inner smile as she mentally crossed her fingers over the fact that the song hadn't yet been written. Hoping that she wasn't tampering with future events, she softly began to sing the words that had given her more strength in recent few weeks than ever before.

"I believe in Christ; he is my King!
With all my heart to him I'll sing;
I'll raise my voice in praise and joy,
In grand amens my tongue employ.
I believe in Christ; he is God's Son.
On earth to dwell his soul did come.
He healed the sick; the dead he raised.
Good works were his; his name be praised."

Tyler stared as the final strains of Amber's song faded away. This was something else he hadn't known about her. She had the voice of an angel. He swallowed the lump in his throat that had formed when Amber had started singing and closed his eyes against the images the voice evoked. He knew another woman who had the voice of an angel. His mother. She had sung him to sleep when he was young. How had he forgotten?

Following the service, Tyler, Amber, and Ian were treated to a large German lunch. Amber devoured every detail of the Dietrichs' story—their conversion and subsequent immigration to the States. They had plans to join the rest of the Saints out west when their son and his family were able to travel from Germany to be with them.

It was with some reluctance that the well-fed trio left the cozy comfort of the small home. The ride back to the camp was a quiet one. As they neared their destination, Amber gave in to the feelings of curiosity she'd experienced about Ian since meeting him. "I have to ask you something," she finally said, turning to him.

"Yes?"

"How is it that you're here, and not out west with the rest of the Saints?"

Ian smiled. "My mother and I joined the Church when I was young. As I mentioned before when we talked about my family, my father didn't approve, but he didn't object either. Obviously, she was not in a position to join with the other Saints moving west and still keep her marriage intact. She died shortly after I was baptized. My father allowed me to stay in contact with some of the other members that were still in the area. I was ordained later by a couple of missionaries who were traveling west, having been in England for five years."

He paused, reflecting. "My father is a very patriotic man. He promised me that if I did my duty to my country, he would let me teach him about the gospel."

Tyler abruptly brought his and Amber's horse to a halt. "You're telling me that you're risking your life in this hellish place just so your father will hear the details of your faith?"

"Yes," Ian smiled.

"And he didn't promise he'd join your church?"

"No, he didn't."

"So you're basically living on hope," Tyler prodded.

Ian's smile grew. "Basically, yes."

Tyler shook his head and nudged the horse into motion. "I just don't get it," he mumbled.

Amber had remained silent, attempting to gauge Tyler's mood. When they returned to camp, Amber broached the subject again. "Tyler, do you think I'm an intelligent person?"

He regarded her quizzically. "Of course I do. You know that."

"Well then, do you honestly think I would devote my life to a bunch of nonsense?"

He offered no reply, so she ventured forward.

"I know it's true, Tyler. I know it is. I've had too many answers to prayers, personal prayers, to believe otherwise." They sat in silence for a while. She finally added, "It's a feeling, more than anything. You can't 'prove' it's true to anyone."

Tyler shrugged. "It's okay, Amber. I'm not asking for proof of anything."

She studied him for a moment, wishing she could read his thoughts. "Do you really not believe in God?"

His shoulders slumped slightly and he looked tired. "I suppose I do. I think he's just too busy doing God-like things to notice the little people."

She opened her mouth to voice a protest when a corporal materialized seemingly out of nowhere and saluted Tyler. "The general needs to see you at once, sir," the boy said.

"Fine, I'll be right there." He waited until the soldier had left, then approached Amber. Planting his hands on her shoulders, he drew her toward him to kiss her forehead. "Don't try to figure me out, Amber. It's much too messy." He moved to leave, then turned back to add, "Your song—it was beautiful."

****

The word spread like wildfire. The Pennsylvania Fourth Artillery regiment was engaged in battle approximately seven miles to the east. Amber was summoned to the medical station as several hundred troops prepared to move in as back-up. The medical team quickly packed the supplies they could manage to move on such short notice and rode out behind the soldiers. Amber was gone before Tyler knew she was leaving.

The battle sight that greeted Amber was a gruesome one. The medical station was set up at the back of the battlefield and scores of wounded soldiers were carried there, moaning and crying out for help. Her mind flew in a million different directions as the atmosphere assaulted her senses. She spied a few women boiling gruel over a fire for the men to eat, and absently wondered if one of them might be what one man had once referred to as "the angel of the battlefield"— Clara Barton herself.

She never got the chance to ask; instead she adjusted quickly and began the ghastly "operating" process. She had been contemplating the fact that she might encounter battlefield surgery and was modifying the crudity of the situation as best she could.

She saw many cases where bullets had shattered bones or split them for several inches. The soldiers were often ill prior to their injuries and did not have the physical stamina required for any kind of limb-saving efforts or complicated surgery. Perhaps in her own time, Amber could have properly set the breaks and would have had time for complex efforts. As it was, she considered herself lucky to have more than just a few minutes with each wounded man. Her time was split between her own ministrations and somewhat futile efforts to instruct her colleagues.

There were two basic limb-removing techniques being used by the medical team, both of which were actually variations of techniques she had been taught herself. She was, however, horror-struck to observe some of the less-experienced physicians beginning with the first technique, only to carve away too much tissue and attempt to close the surgical process with a variation of the second technique.

She observed other inept procedures that were begun improperly and left bone protruding as the end result. Wanting to scream in frustration, she attempted to offer suggestions without appearing authoritative and worked as fast as she could do so effectively.

She tried not to look at the growing mound of amputated limbs and blocked out the offending smells and sounds. The medical team worked mechanically for several hours before the line of soldiers dwindled and the maniacal pace slowed.

Amber had just washed her red, chapped hands and with a stick lifted a few surgical instruments out of a kettle of boiling water when she felt an unsettling sensation tickle the back of her neck. She raised her head and looked around, scanning the battlefield for the cause of her discomfort. Dropping the surgical instruments back into the kettle, she ventured forward, not really knowing why.

"Hey! Dr. Saxton, where are you going?"

Amber barely spared the young medic a backward glance as she ventured forward onto the battlefield. For all intents and purposes, the battle itself was over; the only remnants of the enemy were those who lay maimed or dead.

She picked her way among the death and debris, distressed by the weak calls for help and the horror strewn about in abundance. She fought rising waves of nausea; as much as she'd seen as an ER doctor, nothing could have prepared her for the devastation she witnessed.

What am I doing? she thought as she stared down into the sightless eyes of a dead Union soldier. She shook her head in hopeless confusion, and turning to make her way back to the relative safety of the medical station, spied a small movement to her left—barely enough to recognize.

Her world came to a halt as her focus narrowed in on the fallen soldier's face. Her legs wouldn't obey her command to move—she stood rooted to the spot even as her mind willed her body into action. Finally rescued by instinct, she stumbled to the soldier and fell to her knees at his side.

"Oh, Boyd." She felt what was left of her professional exterior melt as tears filled her eyes. For the boy's sake, she sternly chastised herself and tenderly brushed his hair from his forehead. "What on earth have you been doing?" she whispered, forcing a tremulous smile.

"Dr. Saxton." Boyd's relief was visible. "I'm afraid I'm not doing too well."

Amber had to silently agree as she opened his shirt and surveyed the damage done to his abdomen. She lifted her head and searched desperately for someone to help her move the stricken young man. In the distance, she saw Ian walking rapidly toward her with Tyler close behind.

She spoke quietly as the twosome ventured within earshot—"I need a stretcher. Now."

Chapter 20

A mber situated Boyd as comfortably as she could manage on an "operating table" when he was transported back to the medical station.

"I'll be back in about two seconds, Boyd. I promise I won't be
long." Amber pulled Ian off to one side and whispered urgently, "You
are an elder, aren't you?"

He nodded.

"If Boyd agrees, will you administer to him?"

"What's administer?" Tyler was trying to follow the conversation.

"It's a blessing. Like a special prayer," Amber offered hastily by
way of explanation.

Ian nodded in response to her question. "Of course. Can you
help him?"

Amber felt her composure slip again. "His wounds are so bad. If I
were operating on him back home, he might have a chance." Despite
her best efforts, tears slipped from her eyes and rolled down her face.
"I'm exhausted. I don't have the right equipment. I can't do this alone."

Ian didn't hesitate. "Come on." He led the way back to the crude
table where Boyd lay bleeding. He asked Boyd if he'd object to the
blessing.

"I'd be honored, sir," came the faint reply.

"Hurry," Amber said quietly and began prepping the young soldier for surgery. *I'm sure the Lord won't mind,* she thought to herself, *if
I work while the blessing is being said.*

"What's your full name, Boyd?" Ian asked as he gently placed both
hands on the boy's head.

"Weldon Boyd Saxton."

Amber's busy hands stilled, and she looked in astonishment at Boyd's face. He closed his eyes as the blessing began and missed Amber's expression.

The familiar phrases and the cadence of Ian's voice washed over her mind and provided her a great measure of comfort. The blessing was simple—that the will of the Father be done and the hands of the surgeon be blessed.

Saying little, Amber worked feverishly the next three hours. She communicated with the physician who kept Boyd anesthetized by dropping small amounts of ether through a clean cloth and into the mouth of the patient. She had recruited Dr. Davis to stand with her and assist as needed, which he did willingly and without complaint. She felt direction and inspiration flow through her mind and into her hands as she repaired the damage as best she could.

Amber finished her work, satisfied with her results and grateful to see that her patient was still resting comfortably. Only as she began to again tune into reality did she realize she'd had an audience. Her medical colleagues had gathered to watch her perform what, to them, seemed magic. She spent some time answering questions and seeing to Boyd's security inside a makeshift infirmary tent where the most seriously wounded were resting. Before long, she found herself at the foot of Boyd's cot with only Ian and Tyler, everyone else having dispersed to see to separate duties.

"Believe it or not," Ian was saying, "this was actually a relatively small battle. I've seen some twice this bad. I understand the general is ecstatic," he said grimly. "This will go down as a win for his regiment."

Amber indulged herself with a fantasy wherein she scratched the general's eyes out. He *would* see the battle as only a victory, she seethed, and probably not lament the loss of his own men other than to be disappointed in his reduced numbers. She rubbed her eyes. "I need to get some rest now while I can. I'm staying here for tonight, at least." She looked at the men as though she expected an argument. They didn't give her any.

"Where will you sleep?" Tyler asked her quietly.

"Over there." She pointed to an empty space on the ground next to Boyd's cot.

Tyler nodded. "I'll check on you in the morning." He kissed her cheek and gave her a brief hug. "I'm proud of you," he whispered in her ear.

Amber smiled. "Thanks." She touched Ian's arm as the men turned to go. "I can't thank you enough, Ian. I couldn't have done it otherwise."

"It wasn't me, Amber," Ian said. "You know that."

****

After Tyler and Ian left, Amber collapsed on her knees in solitude behind the walls of the makeshift infirmary. Her stores of adrenaline depleted, her bottled emotions escaped the confines of her body in rasping sobs. The effort to hold herself upright became herculean and beyond her capacity to endure. She touched her forehead to the earth, her shoulders shaking as unbidden tears fell from her eyes, creating damp circles in the dry dust inches from her face.

You will render service through your chosen profession that will prove invaluable to your family for generations on end. The line from her patriarchal blessing repeated itself in her mind as she released the tension and fear she'd felt since before she'd spied Boyd, *her ancestor*, collapsed on the field of battle. Never in a million years would she have imagined that in fulfilling that prophecy in her blessing, she'd be saving her own line. Had Boyd died before he married and had children, it would have been necessary for her to be born through a different line altogether. He was the last living child of his mother with no other immediate relatives. She thought of her parents, her family, the things she'd learned from them, and was so overwhelmed at the part she'd played in keeping the whole of it intact that she felt faint.

"What if I had failed?!" Her mind fairly screamed the horrified thought as she sobbed, but the words themselves came out on a hoarse, choked whisper. *Father, what if I had failed?*

The racking sobs gradually subsided as Amber felt exhaustion fully overtake her limbs. She wondered vaguely about her ability to rise from her position on the ground and return to the infirmary where Boyd lay sleeping. When she was sure she'd never be able to summon the strength to move, a calm and gentle peace stole over her heart. *All is well. All is well.*

She'd sung the sweet strains of "Come, Come Ye Saints" in church meetings for as long as she could remember. The fact that she heard the words to the chorus in her mind as she lay humbled and weary on the hard earth came as no real surprise. She did not question their source; she managed a misty smile of gratitude as she lifted her head from the ground and made her way slowly into the infirmary to her healing patient.

****

Tyler and Ian rode to the general's makeshift headquarters, approximately one-half mile away from the battle site, in relative silence. When he could stand it no longer, Tyler turned to Ian and said, "Okay. I want to understand what happened today."

"What exactly would you like to know?"

"Well, according to Amber, Boyd would have died if you hadn't said that prayer."

Ian was quiet for a moment. "It's hard to understand it without some appreciation for God and Jesus Christ." He paused. "You're not religious at all, are you." It was more of a statement than a question.

Tyler shook his head.

"Well, is it all right if I give you a little background about our church before I try to explain the blessing?" he asked cautiously.

"Sure, whatever."

One hour of discussion became two, and then three. The two men sat outside under a blanket of stars, enjoying the peaceful surroundings as they conversed. As Tyler listened carefully to the stories of Joseph Smith and the Book of Mormon, he tried to remain objective. He was a rational person, after all, he told himself, and he'd been away from his own reality for too long.

That had to be the reason, certainly, that the thought of a fourteen-year-old boy seeing God and Jesus Christ wasn't completely ridiculous. In his soul, he recognized it as truth. The Book of Mormon, Ian's explanation of the priesthood, the blessing he'd witnessed—it all felt right. He'd long wondered about the notion of insanity running rampant through his family; this just might be the proof he'd needed, he mused wryly.

Ian yawned, prompting Tyler to glance guiltily at his companion. "I'm sorry. I've kept you talking forever. I'm sure you're tired. I know I am."

"Please don't apologize. I've enjoyed myself." Ian stood stiffly and stretched his arms above his head. "In fact," he said, "I think I know what I'll do after the war. I'd like to serve a mission."

"Well, you're very effective." Tyler stood and the two men shook hands. "Thank you, truly, for your time tonight. I . . ." He trailed off, unsure of exactly what it was he wanted to say.

"You're welcome." Ian turned and retrieved two small books from his saddlebags. "You may be interested in reading these. I borrowed this one back from Amber, and the other is what we call the Doctrine and Covenants. They're revelations given to the Prophet Joseph and others."

Tyler looked down at the books Ian handed to him and smiled. "I suppose I have some reading to do."

As Ian disappeared to prepare for bed, Tyler looked impatiently about himself. The men were all sleeping under the stars and he had no tent for privacy. His mind was too full of thoughts and emotions that tumbled and bounced around, giving him little peace and making it impossible to sleep. He lit a lantern, and clutching the small books in one hand, walked off into the trees toward the sound of running water. He hadn't gone far when he found the source of the noise; a small river that was close enough to the camp for safety's sake, yet far enough away to afford him some solitude. He found a spot on the ground that was level enough to sit with the lantern and books.

He flipped through the pages of the Book of Mormon, not knowing what he was looking for. Finally deciding to begin at the beginning, he read the first line, then closed the book, dropping it on the ground next to him. "It must have been nice for you, Nephi, to have been born of goodly parents," he said aloud into the cold air. The night was perfectly still as his thoughts swirled about in his head.

"Why couldn't you have given me goodly parents?" he whispered in anguish toward the heavens. The tears formed slowly and soon cascaded down his tired face. "Don't you know what my life has been like? Where were you when I needed you? When my sister and mother needed you? I really could have used a good father!" Tyler hung his head and released the agony he'd buried for years. Through blurred vision he saw tears falling on and rolling down the front cover of the second book Ian had given him, which was resting on his lap.

Open the book. The soft impression stole quietly into his aching mind and asserted itself once again. *Open the book.* He lifted it and listlessly opened the front cover, holding it flat against his palm. A soft breeze wafted through the trees and across the river, rifling the pages of the book as it traveled. Section 78. The pages stopped moving, and as Tyler gazed at the words, all seemed blurred but a few lines, which he read silently through his tears. *Verily, verily, I say unto you, ye are little children, and ye have not as yet understood how great blessings the Father hath in his own hands and prepared for you: And ye cannot bear all things now; nevertheless, be of good cheer, for I will lead you along. The kingdom is yours and the blessings thereof are yours, and the riches of eternity are yours.*

Tyler stared through his tears down at the book resting gently in his hand, hardly daring to breathe as the breeze once again lifted the pages and came to rest on the section entitled 121. Again, two sentences stood out above the rest: *My son, peace be unto thy soul; thine adversity and thine afflictions shall be but a small moment; And then, if thou endure it well, God shall exalt thee on high; thou shalt triumph over all thy foes.*

A warm feeling of love and comfort settled over his mind and heart, and he slowly ran his fingers over the precious words as though they were tangible. The tears continued to flow, although the reason for their existence had become twofold. His pain hadn't disappeared, but it was a good start. He sat for a long time before the words finally formed on his lips.

"Thank you," he whispered softly into the night.

Chapter 21

Pleased with his progress through the night, Amber sat by Boyd's bedside and softly brushed his hair off his forehead. She hadn't slept well for fear his condition would worsen, but the night had passed uneventfully. He eventually stirred and his eyelids fluttered, his eyes coming into focus on Amber's concerned face.

She smiled. "So how's my favorite patient feeling?"

Boyd winced as he attempted to shift his position on the narrow cot. "Awfully sore, ma'am."

"Try to stay still for a while. I'll give you something for the pain." Morphine was not accepted as an appropriate painkiller yet, and as such was hard to come by. When she had happened upon some while going through discarded medical supplies, she had grabbed it as though it were gold. S. Weir Mitchell was a neurologist during the Civil War who worked with patients suffering from paralysis. Amber remembered reading a textbook in college that showed Dr. Mitchell had been very much in favor of morphine use. She supposed she had him to thank for its existence in the medical supplies.

"Can I have some whiskey?" Boyd whispered.

"Absolutely not," Amber said. "I have something much better. I don't want you drinking even a drop of alcohol, is that clear?"

"Yes, ma'am."

Amber gently held his limp hand and gazed into his face. "Why didn't you tell me, Boyd?"

"Ma'am?" he wondered.

"That we share the same last name."

Boyd was still for a moment. "I don't know, exactly," he finally replied. "I don't talk much. I was too embarrassed to mention it to you, I guess." He hesitated, the blush spreading across his face more pronounced because of his pale, pain-induced countenance. "You're so smart and beautiful. I always feel so shy around you."

"Oh, Boyd. You are so sweet. I think you're wonderful." Amber was overwhelmed by the moment. She couldn't remember a time in her life when tears had been so readily accessible as they had been recently. She cleared her throat. "You know, my father's name is the same as your first name. He told me that he was named after an ancestor who immigrated here from England."

"Well, that's a coincidence. My great-grandfather's name was Weldon Saxton, and he brought his family here from England shortly after the Revolution." Boyd smiled weakly. "Maybe we're related, ma'am."

"I'm sure we probably are, Boyd. Please call me Amber."

****

Every minute of the three weeks that followed the battle was consumed by marching as the regiment moved closer to Vicksburg, Mississippi, in preparation for an invasion. Since diseases continued to spread, sick patients kept Amber and the medical team busy at night. She counted her blessings daily; among them was the fact that she and Tyler had been able to avoid contracting any diseases. Tyler was so involved in meeting the general's incessant demands that he and Amber hadn't spent any substantial time together since before the battle.

It was with some desperation that Tyler pleaded an illness to the general one evening as the regiment neared its destination and was relieved of his duties for the night. He wandered to the medical unit and sat down inside the tent at the end of a relatively short line of ailing soldiers. Amber was working with the medical staff and didn't notice him until his turn in line came and he planted himself squarely on an overturned barrel in front of her.

"I have to talk to you tonight," he said without preamble.

"Hello to you too, Major," she said with a wry grin.

"This is ridiculous," he hissed quietly. "It's been forever since I've seen you, and I have something to tell you. My evening is free. How soon can you get out of here?"

She sobered instantly. "What's wrong? Tell me now."

"I can't tell you now." He sounded exasperated. "How soon can you leave?" he repeated.

She looked around at the soldiers. "Wait here."

Tyler sat impatiently while Amber conversed with Dr. Davis. She finally returned, pulling her cloak on as she walked. "Let's go," she said. "It seems I have the evening free too."

They left the tent and stepped into the cold night air. "Where are we going?" Amber asked as she pulled her hood up over her head.

Tyler shoved one hand into the pocket of his overcoat and pulled her close with the other arm. "This way," he said, and led her quickly to his tent. He ushered her inside, lit a lantern and motioned to his bedroll. "Sit down," he said, and then sat opposite her after bundling her in a wool blanket.

"Okay. What's going on?"

He took a deep breath. "Several things. First, this." He took her face in his hands and kissed her thoroughly, completely catching her by surprise and leaving her more than a little breathless.

She looked dazed and completely disappointed when he drew back. He laughed. "Don't look at me like that, or I'll never tell you everything I need to."

She sighed and smiled. "Okay. Talk away."

"I'm going to ask Ian to baptize me."

She dropped her jaw in stunned silence, her eyes huge. "What—what—how—" was all she managed to say.

He quietly related his experiences with the scriptures on the night of Boyd's surgery. "I've been reading the Book of Mormon," he finally finished. "It just feels right. Amazingly enough, I've felt more at peace in these past few weeks than I've ever been." He smiled ruefully. "Even in the midst of all this." He motioned to the surrounding camp they both knew lay beyond the thin walls of the tent.

Amber tried to swallow past the lump that had risen in her throat. "Tyler," she whispered as tears escaped her eyes and rolled down her face. "I don't know what to say."

He gathered her into his lap and held her close. "I love you so much, Amber," he whispered, gently rubbing her back. "Not a moment goes by that I don't want to be with you. When we get home, I want you to marry me."

She choked out a laugh through her tears. "Is that an order?" Grinning, she pulled back to watch his sheepish expression. "That's not fair, you know. I tried to tell you weeks ago that I loved you, and you wouldn't let me."

"Ah, yes. That would have been our conversation during my drinking binge." He winced.

"Yes, that would be the one."

"Well, I really don't mind if you say it now," he said. "In fact, I rather wish you would."

She smiled. "Of course I love you. You know I do." She wrapped her arms around his neck and hugged him tightly. "And, not that you *asked*, exactly, but yes, I will marry you."

He nuzzled his face against her neck and smiled. "Good. I'd hoped you'd see it my way." He was silent for a moment, sobering. "There's something else we have to talk about."

She groaned. "I knew there was something wrong."

"Not wrong, exactly," he hedged. "We have a chance to find out what the general is up to."

"Great!" she exclaimed.

He hesitated. "You may not think so in a minute. Do you remember when we overheard Edwards talking to the Southern officer that day near Vicksburg?" Amber nodded. "Well, the general wants you to be the messenger at the ball they mentioned. The only reason I don't mind is because I have permission to trail you."

Amber slowly nodded. She had decided after the battle that her role in Boyd's surgery had to be one of the primary reasons for her presence there. She could only speculate on Tyler's role in the whole thing; she suspected that he might find some sense of peace if he could deal with the issues he'd ignored when his father was alive.

"Then we could figure out what's going on," she said. "That must be one of the reasons we're here."

Tyler nodded. "That's my guess. Anyway, the general said he wants to ask you about this himself, so act surprised. You may also want to be a little reluctant. We don't want him to be suspicious."

Amber nodded. "When is he supposed to talk to me?"

"Tomorrow."

****

Amber entered the general's tent dreading his probing eyes and the leering smile she had come to expect. She cleared her throat. "You sent for me, sir?"

He turned at the sound of her voice. "Ah, Amber," he said smiling, extending his hand to her. "Please, sit down with me for a moment." She stepped forward and forced herself to take his hand. He guided her to a wooden chair and sat opposite her behind his desk.

"You're looking well, as usual. I must say, your sojourn into the battlefield has not detracted from your beauty in the least." He reached across the desk and raised her hand to his lips.

She willed herself to meet his devouring gaze and remain cordial. "Oh, sir. You flatter me."

"Not at all."

Amber gently but insistently tugged at her hand, which he still held firmly within his own. He smiled and released his hold. "I'll come right to the point, Amber," he said, reaching for his coffee mug on the desk. "I need you to do something for me. A favor." He took a long swallow and she waited patiently for him to finish. He set the mug down and leaned back in his chair, folding his arms across his chest. "Would you be willing to help me?"

Amber met his gaze. "I suppose it would depend on what you're asking of me."

He chuckled, regarding her closely. "I don't intimidate you at all, do I, Amber." It was actually more of a statement than a question. She gave him a small smile, but said nothing.

"Men jump at my commands and women inconvenience themselves to do my bidding. I'm afraid I have a rather harsh reputation." His lips formed a smile that didn't reach his eyes. "What is it about you that is so different?"

"I'm not sure I understand what you're saying, sir," she lied. "I find your company most enjoyable."

He regarded her for a long, intense moment. Amber locked her eyes into his piercing gaze and didn't flinch or blink.

"You're a smart woman, Amber. You would do well to remain on favorable terms with me." He took another sip of his coffee, not really expecting a reply.

"What is it, exactly, that you want from me, General?"

"I need you to act as a messenger of sorts," he said. "I know, we have other messengers. Unfortunately, those men would look ridiculous in a ball gown."

Amber raised her eyebrows. "You want a woman to act as a spy for you?"

The general gave a short laugh. "'Spy' is such a severe word. All I need you to do is attend a party in honor of General Morris' daughter. She has just turned eighteen years old, and I'm sure her mother is frantically trying to find a suitable husband for her. Some things don't change, even during war."

"General Morris is a Confederate."

Montgomery smiled. "Yes, he is."

"Sir, I'm sure I don't need to tell you that this whole suggestion makes me nervous," Amber said. "I'd rather operate on the battlefield than pose as a Southern belle at a debutante ball."

"Amber, I've known you for quite a while now," said the general. "You've proven yourself to be not only beautiful, but also charming and levelheaded, even in the most dire of circumstances. All you will be required to do is attend the ball, locate a man named Hawthorne, and discreetly accept a small piece of paper he will offer you."

"How long would I have to stay?"

"Long enough to meet with Hawthorne, and maybe dance with a soldier or two," he said. "Looking like you do, if you merely run in and run out again, you'll cause a stir."

"I'll cause a stir if I stay," she said. "My accent would be a dead giveaway!"

"I'm sure you can manage a Southern drawl for an hour or two." The challenge in the general's voice was unmistakable. "After all, you were bright enough to finish medical school, yes?"

Amber bit back a sarcastic retort. Instead, she scrambled to continue her apparently reluctant attitude. The prospect of discovering what the man was doing was tantalizing, to say the least, and she didn't want him to become suspicious. "But sir, I have nothing to wear."

"Amber, you surprise me. I assumed that a woman of your courage and intellect would appreciate a civilized venture into enemy territory."

"General, I am not naïve enough to believe I would receive merely a slap on the hand, should my true purpose be discovered," Amber stated. "Spies are not dealt with kindly, and contrary to what you obviously believe, I am not immune to fear."

The general leaned forward and grasped her hand. "You will not be 'discovered.' Create a false history. Tell everyone that you're from Atlanta, visiting your dear aunt in Mississippi. I have the invitation you'll need to gain admittance." He patted her hand and released it, giving her a sly smile. "I have also taken the liberty of having a dress made for the occasion. That should please you."

Amber shook her head slightly in disbelief. *Placate a woman with clothing*, she thought in disgust.

Montgomery's eyes narrowed. She noticed his change of expression and realized she had spoken her thoughts aloud. She smiled at him and said, "Of course I will help you. Anything for the preservation of the Union."

"Indeed," he murmured.

"When is this party?"

"Tomorrow night."

Chapter 22

"O'Brian! Over here!" Ian followed the urgent whisper that led him behind the general's tent. He found Tyler crouched down in the shadows.

"What are you doing?" Ian's incredulity was clearly etched in his handsome features.

Tyler motioned for Ian to join him. "I'm waiting for the general. I'm hoping to overhear his conversation with Edwards."

"But why?"

"I can't explain everything now, but I need your help. The general is up to something Amber and I are pretty sure is illegal. I want you to know about it, whatever it is, in case something should happen to me or Amber."

Ian started in surprise. "Is something going to happen?"

"I don't know. We may suddenly . . . disappear," Tyler said.

Ian looked alarmed. "What on earth are you talking about?"

Tyler contemplated his answer for a while before he spoke. "This will sound crazy, Ian. I'm not sure what you'll think of me after I tell you."

"Come now, how bad can it be?"

Tyler took a deep breath. "Amber and I fell asleep in the year 1999 and woke up in 1862 at the hospital in D.C. We're about 137 years away from home."

The silence deepened as Ian warily eyed Tyler. "This is madness," he finally whispered.

"Think about it, all of it, from the beginning," Tyler said. "Don't we seem a bit odd to you?"

Ian appeared to contemplate the matter for a moment, looking intently into Tyler's eyes as if searching for the truth, before he reluctantly nodded. "I believe you, amazingly enough." He paused. "Can you answer just a couple of questions for me?"

"Sure."

"Will we ever win this war?" Ian held his breath as though he dreaded the answer.

Tyler gave him a pained smile. "Yes, but not until 1865, I think. In fact," he added, "Abraham Lincoln will sign the Emancipation Proclamation in January of 1863. That's next month. The slaves will be free."

Ian closed his eyes. "I can't tell you how wonderful that is to hear." He was quiet for a moment. "One more thing."

"What is it?"

"Does the Church thrive?" Ian's expression was hopeful and expectant.

"I should say so. Over ten million members, I think Amber said. I was going to ask you to baptize me . . ." He stopped speaking as voices approached. The general and Major Edwards entered the tent, engaged in serious conversation. Their voices were low, and the two men huddling outside strained to hear. As the dialogue progressed, Ian's eyes widened in shock and Tyler shook his head in disgust.

"I should have guessed," Tyler muttered as the general and Edwards left the tent in search of Amber.

"I don't believe it." Ian was stunned.

"Well, I do," Tyler retorted. "I forgot to mention something. That man is my great, great, great, great, great, great-grandfather."

****

Amber nervously paced back and forth in front of her tent, taking care not to drag her voluminous skirts in the mud. Her stomach churned with anticipation as she spied the general approaching.

"Once again, may I just say you look absolutely stunning, my dear." The general took one of her gloved hands and kissed it. "When you return tonight, I'd like you to report directly to me. I'll be in my tent. Don't bother changing your clothes."

"I don't think . . ." She broke off and breathed an inaudible sigh of relief as Tyler and Ian joined them. The general glanced at Tyler with barely concealed annoyance.

"One of our southern counterparts will accompany Miss Saxton," the general stated flatly, "and you may follow discreetly behind," he finished, looking at Tyler. "You must keep your distance, however, and not approach Miss Saxton at any time. Am I clear?"

"Yes, sir."

"Good." They all turned at the sound of hoofbeats to see a young man dressed in a Confederate uniform sitting at the reins of a small, open carriage drawn by two horses.

"General Montgomery?" The young soldier stepped from the carriage.

"Here is your passenger." The general propelled Amber toward the carriage. "You have your instructions," he said to her by way of farewell.

She nodded. Tyler stepped forward to help her into the carriage. "I'll be right behind you," he whispered. Feeling helpless, he stepped back and watched her ride off.

"I never got a chance to tell her what we overheard," he muttered quietly to Ian as he mounted his horse.

"I'll keep an eye on things here," Ian assured him. "Good luck."

****

Amber stared in amazement as the carriage progressed down the tree-lined path toward her destination. The mansion was enormous and fulfilled her every expectation. The night air was clear and cool, the house ablaze with lights and humming with the activity of several hundred people.

The carriage came to a halt at the front of the steps, and Amber smiled at the soldier who had said very little on their journey despite her attempts at conversation. The young man stepped down and offered Amber his hand. He led her up the front steps to the massive doors, bowed, and left.

Amber sighed and stepped inside. She was met by a black butler who offered to take her cloak. She surrendered it reluctantly, fighting the urge to tug upward on the neckline of her gown, which was actually nowhere near her neck. She had to admit the rest of the dress was beautiful. The dark, forest-green satin fell in graceful waves over the enormous and highly cumbersome hoops beneath.

The most difficult adjustment by far, however, was the corset that was laced so tightly she could hardly draw a decent breath. The general had secured the services of a shy young local girl who lived near the camp to temporarily act as a lady's maid. Amber shuddered at the memory of the girl's surprising strength as she had tied the corset securely around Amber's already petite body.

She forced herself to walk steadily toward the French doors that indicated the ballroom. She handed her invitation to the attendant at the door and listened as her alias was announced loudly to the throng within. "Stay close to the door," the general had instructed her. "Hawthorne will find you when your 'name' is announced."

"What will my name be?" she had asked, her eyebrows raised.

"Sarah Elliot." The general looked pleased with himself. "Sarah is my wife's name, and Elliot is my mother's maiden name."

"How utterly charming," Amber said dryly.

The silence had lengthened, and she had grown increasingly uncomfortable as the general allowed his gaze to wander slowly over her ball gown. It was then that she remembered all of Tyler's suspicions that she had never really wanted to believe. *This man is dangerous,* she had realized with a sudden clarity.

Amber was shaken abruptly from her thoughts as she saw Hawthorne walking toward her. She recognized him as Hawk, the man she had seen talking to Edwards that day in the trees. *Another dangerous man,* she thought to herself as he approached. *He's handsome and he uses it to his advantage.*

"Ah, Miss Elliot," Hawthorne exclaimed, bowing over her gloved hand. "How nice to meet you at last. Your journey from Atlanta went well, I trust?"

"As well as can be expected in the midst of this awful war," Amber drawled, slipping easily into the role she'd been mentally rehearsing for hours.

Hawthorne led Amber into the room toward the center where couples were dancing, and as they walked he maintained a steady stream of general conversation for the benefit of any that would over-hear. "And you're enjoying your visit with your aunt?"

"My, yes," she said. "We've been so busy I've hardly had a moment to myself."

They pressed through groups of gaily-dressed people and stopped periodically for brief introductions with various military officers of

Hawthorne's acquaintance. Amber allowed her gaze to wander around the splendor and opulence that were apparent in every detail her eyes could absorb. *But at what cost,* she asked herself sadly as she spied several black slaves situated around the room to serve the guests. She thought of her friend Camille and felt sick.

"Will you do me the honor of this dance?" Hawthorne asked as the strains of a waltz interrupted Amber's troubled thoughts.

"Of course," she answered automatically. "It would be my pleasure."

Amber settled into the rhythm of the dance, having adjusted to the interference of her large dress. She kept up with the pretense of the evening, chattering inanely and smiling at Hawthorne, who was clearly a master at the role of the charming suitor. As they danced and spun, the whole situation took on a surreal feeling for Amber, almost as though she was spinning in slow motion. *Please,* she thought wearily, *Please, I want to go home. I want Tyler and I want to go home.*

The music eventually ended, and Hawthorne drew her arm through his. "You look a bit flushed, my dear. Perhaps we should step into the gardens for a stroll."

Amber nodded. Finally, the moment was at hand. She would get the information and leave. They stepped out onto the balcony and down into the carefully manicured gardens. Hawthorne noticed her shivering as the cold air hit her bare shoulders and arms. He shrugged out of his uniform jacket and placed it around her shoulders. She smiled her thanks and followed him to a secluded corner behind several shrubs. He motioned toward a stone bench and sat next to her.

"Well, well, well, 'Miss Elliot,'" he smirked quietly. "You're a convincing actress. Not bad for a Yankee."

Amber weighed her options. Play dumb, she finally decided.

"The general never tells me anything," she pouted. "I'd like to know what I'm doing here tonight."

Hawthorne smiled and narrowed his eyes. "I could explain everything to you, but then I'd expect a show of gratitude in return for satisfying your curiosity. How much does it mean to you?"

Amber fought a surge of panic. "Well, I'm always the last to know what's going on in that regiment, and for once I'd like to be in on things!"

Hawthorne stroked her cheek with the back of his fingers. "Of course you would, poor thing. A woman's curiosity can be the very devil, can it not? I'd be happy to be the one to tell you everything." He paused, the gleam in his eye predatory and unmistakable. "Well, dear, I hope that what I'm about to say won't be too shocking for your delicate sensibilities."

"Oh sir, I'm very sturdy."

"Mmmm. I can see that, although 'sturdy' probably isn't the word I'd use. Well, enough idle chitchat. General Montgomery recruits Confederate soldiers to monitor the activities of escaping slaves," Hawthorne finally disclosed. "The informants give me the information, and I pass it along to the general. He utilizes his resources to capture the slaves and sell them back to their original owners. He rewards me handsomely for his efforts."

Amber's mind was reeling. She was torn between nausea and disgust, and couldn't control her thoughts.

"You seem surprised," Hawthorne said.

Amber scrambled for composure. "I don't understand why you go through the general. Why not just do it all yourselves and keep the money?"

Hawthorne smiled indulgently. "Because, my dear, the general himself masterminded the whole operation. We can't very well omit him now, can we? Besides which, I don't have access to the resources he does."

Amber was silent, trying to keep the horror she felt inside from manifesting itself on her face.

Hawthorne moved closer to Amber and brushed his fingers lightly across her neck. Amber quickly jumped to her feet and tried to stroll casually back toward the relative safety of the mansion. She caught her breath as Hawthorne laid a heavy arm across her shoulders and propelled her behind a large bush. He pinned her against a waist-high stone retaining wall, his face inches from hers. "Where are you going, Miss Elliot?" he asked.

"I'm cold," she replied evenly. "I want to go back inside."

"But I haven't yet given you what you came for."

Amber held her hand out, palm up. "Let me have it, then."

Hawthorne removed his jacket from her shoulders and extracted a folded piece of paper from the inside pocket, holding it tantalizingly out of her reach. "I believe you promised me a favor in return for enlightening you as it concerns your mission here." His eyes narrowed and she willed herself not to show any fear. "I have a carriage in front and a local cabin at my access. No one would ever know we were gone."

"You know, I'm really feeling awfully sick. Maybe we can do this another time." She closed her eyes in fury as his lips trailed a path down her neck and followed the line of her bodice.

"I'm afraid there won't be a next time," he murmured. "You'll keep your promise to me, and you'll keep it tonight."

"I said I'm not feeling well. I'm sure the whole experience would be something of a disaster if I were to become ill all over you." She had leaned back so far she was bent nearly backward in half over the stone wall. She pushed insistently on his chest to no avail.

"Well, it's certainly convenient that you weren't sick a few minutes ago when you had so many questions about the general. Makes me wonder what your true motives are. How well does the general know you, 'Miss Elliot'?" His hands groped insistently and Amber shoved harder. "I understand he has designs on you himself," he said softly as his lips moved across her skin. "We'll have to keep our little liaisons to ourselves."

"There will be no liaisons! Let me go. Now." Amber fisted her hands in his hair and brought his face up to meet hers. He merely smiled and moved his fingers to grip the edge of her bodice.

"You can come willingly or unwillingly. It makes no difference to me." The glint in his eyes was hard and unyielding, and he moved closer, crushing her painfully against the wall.

"I warned you," she whispered. With her hands still clutching his hair, she smashed the top of her forehead as hard as she could across the bridge of his nose. Her own head ached at the abrupt crack and her eyes smarted with tears, but she was not experiencing nearly the amount of pain as was her captor.

Hawthorne stumbled back and swore viciously, then moved to grab her with one hand while the other cradled his broken face. Amber brought her knee up, and in spite of her layers of skirts and hoops, managed to inflict enough pain on Hawthorne that he stumbled backward yet again and released his grip. Amber snatched the paper that had fallen to the ground, picked up her skirts, and ran as quickly as she could toward the enormous house.

She slipped into the shadows of a clump of bushes and held her breath as Hawthorne raced past her hiding place and into the ballroom. She dashed out from behind the bushes and clung to the shadows of the house, quickly making her way around the corner. She ran along the side of the mansion, hoping she'd make it to the front before Hawthorne realized she wasn't in the ballroom. Her breath came in painful gasps as she tried to draw in as much air as the tightly laced corset would allow. She had almost reached the corner of the front of the house when she was grabbed around the waist from behind. A hand clamped tightly over her mouth as she was hauled roughly up against the house.

Amber began to see splotches before her eyes and knew she was about to faint. She clawed desperately at the hand covering her mouth and elbowed her assailant in the ribs with all her remaining strength. She heard a familiar grunt and whipped her head around as her mouth was released.

"Tyler!" she gasped in surprise.

"Hush!" he hissed and yanked her down to the ground behind another exquisitely manicured bush. He put his arm around her waist and hauled her close up against his side, motioning again for her to keep still. She wearily dropped her head on his shoulder and tried to quiet her erratic breathing.

Two shadowy figures approached from the back of the house, and Amber closed her eyes as she recognized Hawthorne's voice, muffled as though he held a cloth to his face. "She can't be far. I want you to find her. We have some unfinished business to discuss."

Amber cautiously peered out from their hiding place and recognized the boy who had escorted her to the mansion. The plan had been for the young soldier to wait for her out front and take her back to the camp. Tyler and Amber waited until the pair had passed and were well out of hearing range. Tyler whispered instructions, his mouth pressed against her ear.

"We're going to run for the trees over there," he said, gesturing to a large copse approximately fifty yards from their hiding place against the house. "My horse is tied over there. We'll have to share it."

Amber began clawing at the fastenings on the back of her gown. Tyler stared at her in astonishment. "What are you doing?" he whispered furiously.

"I can't breathe," she huffed. "You've got to loosen this blasted corset."

Tyler rolled his eyes. "We don't have time for this," he muttered. They stood and he spun her around, shoving her fumbling hands away from the fastenings at the back of her gown. He quickly found her corset strings and, loosening the knot, pried the whole contraption open a few inches. Amber took a huge breath and smiled.

"Much better," she sighed.

"Hold still," he commanded tersely. He quickly retied the knot and fastened the dress. "Do you have the note?"

Amber showed him the paper she still clutched tightly in her hand.

"Good." He took her hand and looked at her flushed face. "Are you ready?"

She nodded. "Let's go."

They dashed out into the open clearing and ran for the trees, thankfully undetected. Tyler led her through the maze of greenery, finally coming to a stop before his tethered horse. He quickly untied the patient animal and spun around, intending to throw Amber up and into the saddle. He stopped short and exclaimed in an exasperated whisper, "*Now* what are you doing?"

Amber had lifted her skirt up around her waist and was unfastening the enormous hoops that had supported yards upon yards of material. "Do you think there's room for you, me and this wicked contraption on the back of that horse?"

Tyler helped her step free of the hoops and raised a dubious eyebrow at the lacy petticoats and bloomers that covered her legs. "Twentieth-century women should be grateful their clothing is so uncomplicated."

Amber raised her own eyebrows in response. "You know a lot about twentieth-century women's undergarments, Mr. Montgomery?"

"Hey, I had a mother and sister, you know," he said defensively.

"That's a good one," she smirked in response and gathered the volumes of material now hanging limp without the hoops to offer support. Tyler quickly tossed her onto the back of the horse and mounted behind her, jostling her roughly in an attempt to settle into the saddle.

"I will never get used to this," she muttered. "Couldn't you have found another horse?"

He nudged the horse into motion and glared at her. "I didn't think we'd need another one! You were supposed to come back the way you came. I was going to just watch from a safe distance."

Amber glanced up at him, hearing an undercurrent of anger in his voice. "What's wrong with you?"

"What's wrong with me?" Tyler glared down at her as he urged the horse into a full gallop away from the mansion. "What were you thinking when you went outside with that leech?"

Amber was incredulous. "Are you serious? Did you expect him to hand over the information in the middle of a crowded ballroom? We had to go outside." She paused. "How much did you see?"

"I don't know!" Tyler exploded. "I was too far away to get there any sooner. I saw struggling, I saw his slimy hands all over you, and then I saw the most amazing head-butt of my entire life. Are you sure you're okay?"

Amber nodded and took a shaky breath. "You see? I did learn a few things about self-defense. I never thought I'd use it as much as I have these last few weeks, though."

He shrugged out of his jacket and roughly shoved it over her shoulders, covering her from throat to the plunging neckline of her dress. "If you ever wear a dress like this again in public, I swear I'll lock you in a closet! You are not on display, you know—you're going to be my wife, for crying out loud! That's . . . that's mine!" he finished angrily, motioning toward the expanse of her chest not covered by her dress, yet now hidden under the folds of his coat.

"It's not like I had much choice in the matter, you know."

"Well, you could have stuffed a handkerchief down there, or something," he muttered. They rode in silence toward the camp for several minutes before Tyler spoke again. "I am proud of you, though," he admitted gruffly. "You handled yourself well with him."

Amber smiled half-heartedly. "I'm glad you were there."

His lips tightened in fury and his hands shook visibly. "I could kill that man for daring to touch you." Amber closed her eyes and leaned back against his chest. She began shivering uncontrollably. Tyler tightened his arms around her. "Are you cold?"

She shook her head in response. Tyler's brow knitted into a frown and he pulled the horse to a stop. He nudged her chin upward and looked at her closely. "Are you okay?"

She couldn't stop shivering. "I'm fine," she managed in a shaky whisper. "I guess I was more scared than I thought. I know what the general is doing. You're not going to believe this."

"I know. I found out before we left camp. I never got a chance to tell you." Tyler put his hand on her face. "Listen to me. We're meeting Ian about two miles outside of camp. We'll give him the note there and have him pass along everything we know to someone who can do something about it. Then you and I are going to get out of here. We'll leave the country; we'll go to Utah—anywhere."

Amber smiled in spite of herself. "It's not 'Utah' yet. It's still 'Deseret'."

"Whatever. I just know we can't stay around here any longer. I think we've done what we came here to do." He picked up the reins and urged the horse forward. "I may not be able to get us home, but I can at least get us out of this hellhole."

Amber was silent for several minutes. "You're wearing that uniform again . . ."

"I know."

They both looked down at the Confederate uniform he'd obtained in order to be at the mansion and not attract any undue attention. Tyler raised his eyebrows. "I guess I'd better hurry and change my clothes."

"This isn't funny!" She smacked his chest. "We've done what we came here to do! We're probably going to go home soon, but if we can do it without you getting yourself shot, I'd rather go that route!"

Tyler hugged her with the one arm that encircled her waist. "I'll be careful. There's really not much more I can do."

She settled back against him as the horse resumed its pace toward their destination.

"Amber?" His voice was soft against her hair.

"Hmmm?"

"I love you."

She closed her eyes, the emotional pain at the thought of losing him almost incomprehensible. "I love you, too."

Chapter 23

Ian was waiting precisely at the designated location. He looked relieved as Amber and Tyler approached him and dismounted. He moved toward Amber and placed a cloth sack in her hands.

"What's this?" she asked, surprised.

"It's your clothes," Tyler answered for Ian. "We may not have much time, so you need to hurry and change."

Amber nodded and handed Tyler his jacket she had kept close about her shoulders. She clutched her bundle of clothes to her chest and presented Tyler with her back. He deftly unfastened the gown and untied the strings of her corset. Ian averted his gaze as she hurried off a short distance into the trees. He cleared his throat, looking embarrassed.

Tyler grinned. "It's okay, O'Brian. She's going to marry me, you know."

Ian offered his hand and smiled. "Congratulations. It's a good thing, too. Her reputation will be in tatters after traipsing across the country with you."

Tyler sobered as he produced the note Amber had taken from Hawthorne. The two men scanned the contents by the light of a small lantern. The note contained two small bits of information—a location and a number.

"That must be the number of people escaping and the location," Tyler observed. "That doesn't implicate the general, though."

Ian smiled. "While you were gone, the general was, uh, otherwise occupied with a certain local lady in the VIP tent." He paused, looking slightly embarrassed. "So, I searched his trunk."

Tyler raised his eyebrows in surprise. "And you found something? Impossible! I've been searching that trunk for weeks!"

"But did you look carefully? There's a false bottom. My father has a trunk similar to the general's. I used to hide my treasures in it as a child. Well, at any rate, I found these." Ian moved to his saddlebags and extracted several papers rolled together. Tyler whistled softly as he looked over the papers. The general had kept a detailed accounting of the money he received from plantation owners, their names and addresses, and the number of slaves involved in each transaction.

"He was arrogant enough to keep this on his own personal note paper." Tyler shook his head in amazed disgust.

Ian nodded. "Unbelievable, isn't it. General Grant's camp is roughly a two-mile ride from here. I'll give this to him and let him handle things from there. I'll request a transfer, obviously. I can't stay around here any longer. I'd be court-martialed for breaking into the general's property!"

Both men turned as Amber approached wearing her traditional nurse's uniform.

"Did you hear all that?" Tyler asked her. She nodded. Ian mounted his horse, the incriminating documents safely tucked inside his saddlebags. He reached down and shook Tyler's hand, then Amber's.

"I'll miss you both," Ian said, his eyes misting. "Take care," he whispered. He turned his horse and was gone.

Amber took a deep breath and turned to Tyler. "Looks like he thought of everything," she said, motioning to a horse tied to a tree a few feet away from Tyler's own tethered horse.

Tyler nodded as she moved to adjust the stirrups to accommodate the shorter length of her legs. He untied his own horse and waited in silence until Amber was ready to mount.

"Ready?"

She nodded and placed her foot in the stirrup.

"Not so fast." Amber and Tyler whirled around to face the voice coming from the trees. Tyler cursed himself for not extinguishing the lantern as the general and Edwards emerged from the shadows. Still grasping the reins of her horse, Amber inched her way toward Tyler. She stopped beside him and glared at the two men.

The general spoke first. "I certainly hope you're not thinking of leaving the regiment," he said, looking specifically at Tyler. "There are dire consequences for such action, you know."

Tyler returned the general's direct gaze. "Actually, sir, we were just on our way back to camp."

"Oh, really?" Major Edwards sneered, brandishing a rifle. "You were supposed to ride back in the carriage," he said to Amber, "not take off on horseback with him. The soldier showed up without you and was wondering where you were."

"Shut up, Edwards," muttered the general. "And put that thing away. You're going to hurt yourself." He motioned to the weapon Edwards was waving as he spoke.

Edwards opened his mouth to retort and was smoothly cut off. "You disappoint me, Kirk." The general shook his head. "All this time, you've reminded me of myself at your age. Ambitious, hard-working, strong. Unfortunately, though, I'm afraid you're falling short. I'd never have deserted my responsibilities." He turned to Amber before Tyler could reply.

"Where's the message, my dear?" He advanced toward Amber.

"I'm afraid I've lost it," she said. "We've looked everywhere and can't find it."

The general stopped inches from Amber's face. "Give it to me. Now."

"I said," she replied evenly, "I don't have it."

The general moved to grasp her arms when Tyler shoved him and sent him sprawling.

"Hey!" Edwards rushed forward to defend his superior.

"Shut up!" Tyler growled, the look in his eyes so fierce that Edwards retreated a step despite the fact that he held a weapon.

Tyler spun on the general, who was struggling to stand and brush off his clothes. "If you ever come near her again, I'll make you wish you were never born."

"Are you threatening me, soldier?"

"I'm not finished!" Tyler looked at the general through a red haze, seeing only his father. "I despise you. I hate what you did to my mother, to my sister, to me. You ruined my life!"

"You're mad! I don't even know your mother and sister!"

Tyler grabbed the general by the throat and shoved him against a tree. His words came in an angry torrent as the general's eyes bulged. "My mother is an alcoholic now, did you know that? You robbed me of my childhood! You made it impossible for me to trust anyone—I will never, ever forgive you!" Through the fog, he heard Amber's voice.

"Tyler, stop! You're killing him! Tyler, they'll hang you!" She was pulling on his arm in an effort to free the general's throat.

Edwards panicked. He ran into the tangle of bodies and smashed the butt of his rifle against Tyler's head. Tyler immediately fell back, releasing the general and grabbing his head. Edwards turned his weapon around and fired a shot into Tyler's abdomen.

Amber viewed the whole scene with a sense of horror and helplessness. She screamed in outrage as she clutched Tyler from behind, careening backward with him toward the ground. The weight of his body knocked her down, throwing her head back against a rock as they fell. Her last conscious impression was of the warm, sticky blood oozing from Tyler's shirt front and onto her fingers.

Chapter 24

Amber's head was pounding. She opened her eyes and winced at the glaring fluorescent light that illuminated the room from above. She shook her head and tried to focus. She was lying alone on a spare bed in one of the George Washington University Hospital examination rooms.

Her memory assailed her in waves, and she jumped to her feet, grabbing her aching head that screamed in protest at the sudden movement. She ran out of the room and down the hall to the room where she knew Tyler lay bleeding and unconscious. A nurse caught up to her from behind.

"Dr. Saxton," she said breathlessly. "Are you sure you should be up? I hit you pretty hard with that door . . ." The nurse stopped talking and stared. "Did you change your clothes?" She slowed her pace and stopped, watching Amber as she disappeared down the hallway. "How did you change your clothes so fast? We just barely put you in that room!"

Amber ignored the shouting nurse and made her way determinedly toward Tyler's side.

The head resident looked up in surprise as she entered. "Amber, what are you doing?" The pause was deliberate, as was the raise of the eyebrows. "What are you *wearing*?"

Amber looked down absently at her Union Army nurse's uniform as she approached Tyler's side. "I . . . nothing." She picked up Tyler's hand and asked, "How's he doing?"

The doctor looked at her quizzically. "We're taking him up to surgery. What's wrong with you? You were just in here."

"I decided to come back," she said. "Come on, let's get him going."

Amber sat in the doctor's lounge, staring into space at nothing in particular. She had showered, scrubbed her hair vigorously, changed her clothes, and was once again wearing a green scrub suit. The elastic holding her hair in a simple ponytail was an odd contrast to the pins she'd been using for weeks.

She couldn't seem to focus on anything. The irony of the situation wasn't lost on her, however. She had been craving the day when she would return, yet now that it had happened she felt only despair. Tyler would be in surgery for several hours, and even then, the outcome was uncertain.

As she sat, she felt Tyler's voice breaking through the numb fog that seemed to envelop her brain. *Did we make a difference? Did we make a difference? Did we . . .* The thought repeated itself over and over again, until she could no longer sit still.

She stood, grabbed her purse, and ran to the cafeteria, where she hoped she'd find Camille still sitting with Tyler's friend, Derek.

"Can I borrow your car?" she asked Camille breathlessly and without preamble.

"Sure—where are you going?" Camille stood and fished her keys out of her pocket.

"I have to go to the library." Amber took the keys from her friend and, on impulse, hugged her fiercely. "I love you so much." She kissed her smooth, dark, honey-colored cheek and ran for the door, leaving a very confused-looking Camille in her wake.

****

Amber scanned the hundreds of entries on the computer screen listed under the subject "Civil War." She finally typed a name under the sub-topic "Generals." General Stuart Tyler Montgomery. Five titles appeared on the screen. She noted the reference numbers and began her search.

She found the books she was looking for and carried them to a couch in a secluded corner. She found her answer in the first book she opened. Following a brief outline of the general's history and military beginnings Amber found a paragraph that brought tears to her eyes:

The general's military career came to an abrupt halt when a junior officer, Major Ian O'Brian, discovered that the general was orchestrating a slave-capturing organization. Montgomery was court-martialed and found guilty of treason and conspiring with the enemy. He was stripped of all military honors and lived in seclusion until January 4, 1867, when his life ended, due to what modern sources assume was probably severe alcoholism. Major O'Brian was rewarded for his service and diligence to the Union and served under General Grant as a colonel through the end of the war.

Amber couldn't stop the flow of exhausted tears. "We did it," she said aloud. She smiled through her tears as she ran her finger over Ian's name. "We all did it." She took the book to the front desk and checked it out.

****

Amber had been sitting for hours in the doctor's lounge when she finally received the message that Tyler was out of surgery. She quickly made her way to his room and entered, clutching the library book in one hand and Tyler's medical chart in the other.

She approached his bed slowly, finally standing at the edge near his hip. She placed the library book on the bedside tray and grimly scanned the medical charts. She sighed and rubbed her eyes. For the first time in her life, she almost wished she didn't know as much as she did. She would have liked to be able to cling to a bit of foolish optimism.

Tyler's face was deathly pale against his dark hair. Amber gently stroked his cheek and ran her finger lightly over his eyebrows—the same eyebrows that had so many times been raised at her in sarcastic amusement or drawn together in worry or anger. She leaned forward and kissed his cheek, cradling his head in her hands and savoring his nearness and warmth. She closed her eyes as the tears once again escaped and rolled down her face. She sighed and offered the most heartfelt prayer of her life.

Epilogue

Amber gazed at the group of people seated at the banquet-sized table. The reception hall was simply yet beautifully decorated, and the day was perfect. She looked at her husband of one year seated beside her and felt an immeasurable joy swell in her heart.

Tyler felt her gaze and glanced at her. He was listening to the ramblings of Amber's great-aunt seated beside him, and was nodding his head at her observations concerning the recklessness of the youthful generation. He winked at Amber and clasped her fingers with his under the table. She felt the subtle ridge of his garment line against the back of her hand and smiled.

Amber continued her perusal of the group, her eyes moving over the people she loved. Her mother and father. Her sister, Liz, who was seated at her right, trying to choke down her food and disguise her laughter at their crazy aunt. Camille—her best girlfriend and kindred spirit. Tyler's sister, Kristina, who had become a good friend to Amber since her marriage to Tyler. Tyler's mother, sitting quietly with a contented smile on her face. And lastly, Connor O'Brian.

Amber looked at Connor, seated across the table from her and Tyler, marveling again at the beautiful, cobalt-blue eyes that she had seen once before—a long time ago. *Ian would be so proud*, she thought as she looked at the young man who was so handsome and ambitious. She smiled at him in sympathy as her aunt began her inquisition of him for what seemed like the millionth time.

"Now, who are you?" the old woman croaked.

Liz snorted. "Aunt Lucy's in rare form today."

Amber's lips twitched as she nudged her sister. "He's our friend, Aunt Lucy. Do you remember me telling you about him?"

"Yes. Five minutes ago," Liz interjected.

Tyler coughed to cover a laugh and Amber's mother sighed. "Aunt Lucy," she said patiently. "This is Connor O'Brian. He's a friend of Tyler and Amber."

"What's he doing here?" the woman demanded.

Tyler took the reins. "Aunt Lucy, Amber and I have been really into genealogy this past year, and we did some research on Connor's ancestors. We met him after we got married, and he came to live with us for a while."

"What?" Aunt Lucy asked again. "He's living with you? He can't get a job and live on his own?" The old woman was indignant.

Connor put his fork down and cleared his throat. He looked directly at Aunt Lucy with a smile. "I do have a job, ma'am, and I no longer live with Tyler and Amber. I live near them in Virginia."

She continued her inquisition. "Where's your family? Aren't you taking care of your mother?"

Connor looked across the table at the faces of his friends and sighed. They looked back in amusement, letting him wallow alone in his misery. "My family lives here in Utah. In Logan, to be precise, although they're not there right now. My father is a mission president in Brazil." He paused, hoping that the woman would remember this discussion had already taken place. When she merely studied him with sharp eyes, he continued.

"When Tyler and Amber came out here for vacation to do some genealogy, they looked up my family. They knew someone named O'Brian and were helping him do some family research. We all became fast friends, and when Tyler and Amber learned I had just graduated from college and was looking for work, they suggested I might find some good opportunities back east." He looked expectantly at the old woman, hoping the dialogue would be finished. This would be the fifth explanation of his presence since the day had begun.

"Did you serve a mission, young man?"

"Yes, ma'am," he replied. "To England. I'd like to go back sometime soon, but I need to get established with my job in Virginia first."

"Humph," she said. "Don't know why anyone would want to leave this state. Must have broken your poor mother's heart. And Amber and Elizabeth—traipsing all over the country as if they haven't any responsibilities to their poor parents still here at home."

Weldon and Sigrid Saxton looked at each other with raised eyebrows. Weldon glanced down the table at his aunt and said, "We're doing just fine, Aunt Lucy."

"They're barely fifty, for crying out loud," Liz muttered under her breath. She had heard the you-should-be-staying-home lecture from her great-aunt more times than she could count. She looked across the table at Connor and rolled her eyes. Amber caught the exchange and smiled. It wasn't the first time she'd noticed Connor and her sister making eye contact.

Amber looked up when Tyler released her hand, stood, and raised his glass. "I'd like to say something to all of you." He paused as everyone looked his way, then continued. "This past year as Amber's husband has been the happiest of my entire life. I know my baptism and our marriage seemed, well, hasty to put it mildly. When I met Amber in the hospital," he glanced down at his wife and winked, "I knew there was something special about her." He stopped talking for a moment and examined his water glass. "I appreciate your acceptance of me, and your understanding of the fact that I didn't want to wait for a year after my baptism to be married to Amber." He looked at Amber's parents. "I know you must have had your doubts, and I appreciate your faith in me and in your daughter.

"This day is one that we've worked for all year, and the sealing ceremony in the temple this morning was everything I had hoped it would be, and more. To have all of you here to share it with us means more than we can express." He raised his glass. "So, to my beautiful wife, and the people who mean the most to us in the world—all of whom are with us in this room today." He smiled as the group raised their glasses with his.

Aunt Lucy began her rambling again as soon as Tyler sat down. "Still seems crazy to me to get married two weeks after you meet someone. The man nearly dies after being shot by some insane people who broke into his office, falls in love with his doctor and says he wants the missionary discussions while he's still laid up in the hospital and hooked to those beeping machines. And you'd think my nephew's wife would have given her daughter more sense than to run off with some man she barely knew."

Sigrid Saxton sighed again and smiled. "Well, Aunt Lucy, some things just happen quickly. Besides, Amber's always been a bit impulsive. And reckless." She glanced at her daughter with a wink.

"Yes." Tyler put his arm around Amber and nuzzled her ear. "I remember hanging out with my friend Jared in the fifth grade at recess one day when Jared's little sister, Camille, and her friend lost their foursquare ball. Seems to me that Camille's friend couldn't help mouthing off to the bully who'd stolen the ball and said girls couldn't play as well as boys."

He grinned as Amber's jaw dropped open in surprise. "That was *you*! All this time, and you've never said anything . . ."

He laughed. "It's worth it just to see you speechless." He kissed the tip of her nose and smiled.

PHOTO BY ROBERT CASEY

About the Author

Nancy Campbell Allen, a graduate of Weber State University, has dreamed of becoming a writer since early childhood. Her goal is "to provide LDS women with fun fiction that they can read without guilt." In preparation for writing *Love Beyond Time*, which is her first novel, she did extensive research on the Civil War, battlefield medicine, and the day-to-day activities of both North and South armies.

In addition to writing, Nancy enjoys reading, book shopping, traveling, skiing, learning of other times, people, and places, and spending time with her family. She and her husband, Mark, and two children live in Ogden, Utah, where she is a counselor in her stake Primary presidency.

Nancy enjoys hearing from her readers. Visit her website at http://talk.to/nancycallen, e-mail her at necallen@aol.com, or write to her at: PMB #186, 4305 Harrison Blvd., Ogden, UT 84403.